All Along the Watchtower

ALL ALONG THE WATCHTOWER

Curt Colbert

Epicenter Press
6524 NE 181st St.
Suite 2
Kenmore, WA 98028
www. Epicenterpress.com
www. Coffeetownpress.com
www. Camelpress.com

For more information go to: www.epicenterpress.com

Cover Design: Francesca Penchant

Library of Congress Control Number: 2019943853

ISBN: 9781941890684 (trade paper)
ISBN: 9781603811576 (ebook)

Printed in the United States of America

This book is dedicated to all veterans,
especially those vets who suffer from PTSD.

Curt Colbert Published Books

Rat City
Published by UglyTown and Rat City Publishing
2001 & 2014

Rat City
Translation published by Tokyo Sogenshu
2006

Sayonaraville
Published by UglyTown
2003

Queer Street
Published by UglyTown
2004

Seattle Noir / editor
Published by Akashic Press
2008

Under penname Waverly Curtis

Dial C for Chihuahua
Kensington
2012

Chihuahua Confidential
Kensington
2013

The Big Chihuahua
Kensington
2013

The Chihuahua Always Sniff Twice
Kensington
2014

The Silence of the Chihuahuas
Kensington
2015

A Chihuahua in Every Stocking
Kensington / short story
2014

Acknowledgments

I want to acknowledge the help of my dear friend, Waverly Fitzgerald, and our local writing group in the creation of this novel. Also, my thanks for the inspiration and advice gleaned from my local chapter of Sisters in Crime and the local chapter of Mystery Writers of America. And, of course, a big thanks to Phil Garrett and Jennifer McCord of Epicenter-Coffeetown Press for having the faith, and editorial help, in bringing this novel to publication.

Chapter One

"Every soldier must make a compact with himself or with Fate that he is lost. Only then can he function, as he ought to function, under fire. He knows and accepts beforehand that he's dead, although he may still be walking around for a while."

—James Jones: "The Evolution of a Soldier."

They found the dead man sprawled across Jimi Hendrix's grave in the Greenwood Cemetery above Renton, Washington. A white guy in his early fifties, with curly red hair, wearing a leather jacket with a patch on it from the 'Desperados' motorcycle gang. Somebody had carved an old-style peace-symbol deep into the flesh of his meaty forehead. A large button pinned to the corpse's jacket read, *'Are You Experienced?'*

"Why call me about this?" I asked my long-time cop friend, Dale Tanaka, the Seattle Police Department's interagency gang specialist. Busy boy, Dale – worked with various law enforcement agencies over a three-county area. I knew something big must be up for him to phone me from the cemetery before I'd even had a chance to brew my morning coffee.

"Name on the guy's driver's license is Jack Rivers," said Tanaka. "Ring any bells?"

My heart skipped a beat. Jack Rivers had been in too many of my nightmares over the years. "He sure does," I said. "But how'd you know to call *me* about him?"

"We found a list on him. It was pinned to the front of his jacket with that *'Are You Experienced?'* button."

"A list? What kind of list?"

"An Army list," said Tanaka, sounding stuffed up, like his allergies had kicked into high gear. "A personnel roster from 1968. It says, 'First Infantry Division, 2nd Squad, 1st Platoon, Company B.'"

"That's my old unit."

"Yeah, I can see that. Your name's on it, Matt." My adrenaline began to surge as Tanaka continued. "You and seven others. Rivers' too, but his name's been crossed off the list."

"I'll be right out!"

"What the hell is this about?"

I didn't answer. Just slammed down the receiver and red-lined my Firebird all the way to the cemetery.

Fucking Vietnam just wouldn't leave me alone...

...it kept trying to flood in on me as I headed south toward Renton...

...thought I left it all behind thirty years ago – August 20th, 1969 – the day I rotated out, boarded the plane and flew away from the war...

...the best day of my life...

He had always been big and heavy. The years had only made him bigger and heavier. I recognized him immediately. "That's Jack Rivers alright. He was my squad leader in Nam," I told Tanaka.

"Are you sure?"

"You don't forget grunts that machine-gun kids," I told him, thinking that payback's a bitch, considering the four bullet holes that stitched across Rivers' chest.

"Jesus... This have something to do with the war?"

"Has to."

"How?"

"I don't know exactly. It just does," I said.

Tanaka eyed me for a moment. "You're a little pale, Matt. You feel all right?"

"No," I said. "Fuck it. I need to get away from this for a minute. Let's go over and sit in my car; maybe listen to some tapes. I'll fill you in on my history with Rivers."

We crossed the closely mown grass to where I'd parked my vintage '67 Firebird far off to the side of the narrow cemetery access road. Behind us, the graveyard buzzed with early morning activity. Cops, reporters, the evidence team checking over and around Rivers' corpse, taking pictures, making measurements, bagging his hands, etcetera, etcetera, all busily doing the amazing variety of work that had to be done at a crime scene.

Dale and I slid into my car. It was a hot morning, in the mid-eighties already, but I was sweating more than the heat: I was about to tell Dale some things that I didn't like to share.

I was ragged as hell, and lit a smoke. I needed a shower. Needed a shave. Needed some coffee. So, I settled for the Wild Turkey in my glove-box. It would set me straight. It was good. Damned good. Sometimes it even chased the Nam away. I plugged a tape into my eight-track. I always thought better to music. Not one of my favorite Hendrix tapes, though. I didn't much feel like listening to Hendrix, considering the circumstances, and chose another: The Doors: "Light My Fire." Like the Wild Turkey, it was good. But I knew that not even both of them put together would be able to chase the war away today.

"So, Dale," I tried to joke, as the Lizard-King began to sing. "You ready to wallow in the mire?"

"Sounds like that's going to be the case," replied Dale, all serious and business like. "This is some bad shit, isn't it? Talk to me, Matt. How's this guy you were in Vietnam with so long ago end up dead with a list on him that has your name on it? And what the devil is the Hendrix connection?"

"All I can tell you at the moment is about Rivers and me."

"Fine," said Tanaka, taking a swig of my Wild Turkey, something he hardly ever did while on duty. "That's a good place to start."

"Yeah, that's where it started all right," I began, thinking about my screwed up life, my hippie years, all the sex and drugs and rock and roll after I got back from Nam and put flowers in my hair and frigging flowers in my brain, until I got straight and got my P.I. license, then went through three wives while I discovered the benefits of Wild Turkey, and finally realized that the war just wasn't ever going to go away.

"So?" asked Tanaka. "You going to tell me something, or not?"

"I don't like talking about this shit," I said. "But you already know that. So, here goes... I was eighteen when I got to Nam in '68. Greenest cherry you ever saw. Sergeant Rivers went right to work ripening me up. Sent me out on point every day, said he could afford losing a cherry like me more than any of his experienced men. Needless to say, I got experienced really quick." I paused and lit a second smoke off the butt of my first one. "You ever see that movie *Platoon*?" I asked Tanaka.

"Yeah, I saw it."

"You remember the evil Sergeant that Tom Berringer played in it? Crazy, homicidal bastard with all those scars on his face?"

Tanaka nodded. "How could you forget him?"

"Well," I continued. "He was a complete wuss compared to the real thing. Rivers would've eaten him for lunch."

"Bad boy, huh?"

"In spades," I said, starting to walk down that horrible, red dirt road again with my old platoon, as I told Tanaka about Rivers and those kids.

"We were on a search and destroy mission. We'd been ambushed by some V.C. – had a hell of a firefight, then went after them when they broke it off. We chased them to this little village. I was scared shitless. I'd been in country long enough to know that the Cong could be hiding there, blending in with the locals. But I hadn't been around long enough to know what Rivers was really capable of."

"Which was killing kids, huh?" Tanaka asked.

"And everybody else there, including the dogs and a couple water buffalo," I added. "There were about forty people in that village when we went in," I told him. "Only bodies and ashes when we left."

"Jesus..."

"Anyway," I said. "It got even worse in the months to come." I shook my head, trying to clear away the memories. I'd kept them at bay for years. "There were a few of us who didn't like what happened in that village. Rivers told us he'd kill us if we ever said a word to anybody. Bob Oswald, kid from Kalamazoo, Michigan, was the first to try and call Rivers on his threat. But Rivers somehow found out that he was planning to report him to our Company Commander. Bob got fragged out on patrol. He was the only one killed in a short firefight we had. I know he got fragged because Rivers looked me square in the eye when we got back to base camp, smiled and said, 'Too bad about Bob, huh, Rossiter?' I got his message real clear."

"So, nobody ever brought the sonofabitch up on charges?" asked Tanaka.

"No," I said. "I had a chance, once, too."

"How so?"

"Rivers finished his tour of duty almost two months before I did. I thought I could report him once he was gone. But he let everybody know that he would still have eyes and ears in the platoon. Anybody who got ideas would join Bob in a body-bag." I took a deep breath. "So, I kept my mouth shut. All these years. He scared the hell out of me. He still scares the hell out of me."

"I didn't think you were afraid of anything," said Tanaka.

"Everybody's got a few personal demons," I told him. "Nam and Rivers are mine. Then, now and maybe forever."

"I can understand that," said Tanaka, glancing out the window towards the grave site where his men were still busy. "Well, he's dead, Matt," he said, looking back at me. "You don't have to worry about that bastard anymore."

"Yeah," I said, taking a long pull off the Wild Turkey. "Except for one thing."

"What's that?"

"He was the worst stone-killer I ever met," I said, feeling my palms growing sweaty just from talking about him so much. "Whoever killed Rivers has got to be one *bad motherfucker*."

Chapter Two

I didn't get back to my houseboat until almost eleven A.M. I had given Tanaka all the information I could about Sgt. Rivers and our time together in Vietnam. As to what Rivers had been doing, and where he had been living all these years, I didn't have a clue. But I'd do my best to find out. Before I started, though, I needed a shower and shave.

I'd just stepped out of the shower when I heard a noise at my front door. The metal frame around the screen door was loose and it always made a hell of a racket when somebody pulled it open. I expected a knock at the door but only heard the screen rattle and squeak as it shut again.

I quickly wrapped a towel around my waist, pulled my .45 from the holster on my pants, and headed to the front door.

Turned out I didn't need the firepower. Nobody was there. *But there sure as hell had been only a few moments ago.*

I scanned the narrow, floating dock leading up to my houseboat – saw no one, heard nothing except the distant roar of a seaplane landing across the lake. I waited a minute longer, then, still a little edgy, turned to go back inside. That's when I saw it, just inside the screen, taped to my front door: a copy of my old squad list, same as had been found on Rivers' body. Except this one was slightly different – on this list, *my* name was also crossed out.

I wheeled around so fast that I almost knocked my screen door off its hinges. I still saw no one, but could feel eyes on me as surely as the hairs were standing up on the back of my neck. I ducked back inside the houseboat and slammed and locked the door behind me.

I took a nervous glance out the front window: still nobody out there, no movement except the usual few canoes tied up to the long floating dock that snaked back to the wooded shoreline about forty yards distant. *How could someone come and go so quickly?*

I raced across the living room, to check out the rear deck, losing my towel in the process. I edged up beside the sliding-door, then pulled it open and stepped out, pistol at the ready. The deck was empty, save for my two, plastic lawn chairs, gas BBQ, and patio table.

Just then, a young man and woman paddled by, about thirty feet past the deck, in a two-man kayak. The woman saw me, reflexively jerked back from the naked image I presented and promptly capsized the kayak.

Fuck it, I thought. Right now, I could care less who saw me standing here naked.

I got my towel on again and went straight to the phone. I was being targeted, no question. I had a long-standing relationship with one of the best missing-persons people in the business. A local private investigator named Rachel Stern, whom I'd helped train a few years back when she first started out. She'd gone on to become an absolute wizard using computers and the Internet to dig facts and people out of the woodwork. If she couldn't help provide a history on Rivers, nobody could.

Rachel picked up the phone on the second ring. "Stern Detective Agency," she said. "What can I—

"Rachel. It's Matt. Got a minute?"

"That's about all I've got," she told me. "I'm on my way out the door. I've got an appointment with a client."

"With another lovelorn female?" Rachel specialized in doing background searches for women who were dating on the internet.

"This case is a bit more serious," she told me. "I'm doing background research on a sixties radical who went underground."

"Mine's got a sixties connection, too."

I filled her in on the case and told her I needed her help tracking down the members of my old squad.

"Damn, that's terrible," she said. "Of course, I'll help."

"Thanks, Rachel."

"You sure do manage to fall into a lot of these life and death situations," she said. "You ever wonder why?"

"Clean living?"

"Sure," she laughed. "Fax the names and whatever else you've got on them to my office. I'll start digging as soon as I get back."

"I still don't have a fax machine," I said. "Let me give you a couple names now; I'll head to Kinko's and fax the whole list later."

"O.K."

"Numero Uno, is Jack Rivers, my old sergeant. Next is Michael Maloney, our squad's corporal," I said. "He was a real piece of work, too. Let's see," I paused, looking down the list of names – names I'd spent a long time trying to forget. "Henry Baker, Luther Brown and James

Smith. That should be enough to get you started. You'll dig them up in no time."

"Like I'm a magician, right?"

"Yeah, you are. Hour on your computer, you find more info that I can with leg-work half the time."

"You could, too," she told me. "If you ever take the time to learn. This is the Computer Age, Matt; you need— "

"That's why I hire you. I do my thing, you do yours."

"O.K. End of conversation, as usual. Take care. I'll be in touch."

The line went dead. Rachel always got a little miffed whenever I resisted her computer pitch. The last time we had this conversation, I turned it back on her and asked why she didn't learn to use a gun. She told me that was different. That was my thing. And I said, right, that's exactly my point.

Other than that, we got along just fine. Once we'd stopped our brief attempt at dating, that is. I was too old for her, anyway. Just turned the big "5-O," and Rachel was only in her thirties – mid or late, I never asked, and she certainly never volunteered. We worked better together *not* being together, to coin a phrase. Anyway, I needed to get busy.

I slipped on a pair of khaki Dockers and a lightweight maroon Polo shirt that I wore outside my trousers. I holstered my .45 under the shirt at the small of my back. Then I put on my boat-shoes and was ready to go. I never advertised what I did for a living with flashy clothes or attitude. I found it a whole lot more disarming to anyone with potentially bad intentions if I came across as just another unassuming, middle-aged Eddie Bauer type who, like many who had the means, happened to indulge his past youth with a new sports car, or, in my case, a classic muscle-car: a mint '67 Firebird 400 tweaked out at more than five hundred horsepower the way I'd beefed up the engine.

I was going to head over to Kinko's and fax the rest of the names to Rachel, when the phone rang.

"Matt..." It was Tanaka; he sounded agitated. "I need you down here, buddy."

"Down where?" I asked. "Where are you?"

"At the Medical Examiner's office."

"What's up?"

"Your old sergeant had a key lodged in his throat."

"Say what?"

"He tried to swallow a key, and it stuck in this throat. The M. E.

found it. We figured out that it went to one of the storage lockers at the Greyhound Bus Terminal."

"Did you check the locker? Find anything?"

"Yeah, we found something. That's why I need you here."

"What did you find?"

"Part of a body."

"Jesus. What part?"

"A severed head."

"Whose?"

"Don't have a clue. That's why I want you, Matt. Way things have been going, it might be someone you know."

"I'm on my way."

Chapter Three

I didn't like the Morgue. No matter how many chemicals and disinfectants they used, the smell of death was ever present. I had a lot of memories of death. Memories were tough enough to deal with; hard to push aside. Smells, however, were almost impossible to ignore.

As I made my way into the autopsy room, I had this strange, disembodied feeling like I had so often in Nam: I was there, but I wasn't there. All the bad shit happening around me wasn't real, like I'd somehow stepped out of my body and was watching myself slog through it. I guess that made things easier in some way. But it was still a bitch.

I found Tanaka standing next to a stainless-steel table in the middle of the big, stark room. Down at the far end, the Chief Medical Examiner, Doctor Glen Peterson, was hovering over another stainless-steel table, upon which rested the body of a naked, young girl. What I could see of her face, was bruised and battered. Same with the rest of her body. Rough as that was, it was another face that drew my attention; caught my eye so much that I couldn't look away: the face that belonged to the grayish-pink, severed head that lay on the steel table next to Tanaka.

"Hey, Matt," Tanaka said. "You all right? You look off."

"I'm fine."

He studied me a moment, then gestured at the head. "So, do you know this guy?"

"Wish I did."

"You sure?"

"Sure, as I can be." I studied the man's face some more. He looked to be in his forties or early fifties, but I couldn't tell for certain; his face was puffy, spongy, a bit distorted around the eyes and mouth. Try as I might, I couldn't recognize him either as a member of my old squad or anyone else I'd ever met. If he was someone from my unit, thirty-plus years had probably changed him as much as it had me. Like most of the guys my age, I'd put on a few pounds; everything about me had filled out some, including my face. Hell, I hardly recognized myself in pictures taken when I was eighteen or nineteen. How was I supposed to recognize one of the faces from Nam that I'd spent the last three decades trying to forget? Especially one with that all too familiar pallor of death.

"What are these marks on him?" I asked, referring to the whitish spots on the man's nose and ears and cheeks that looked like almost little dried up scars.

"Freezer-burn," said Tanaka.

"Damned if it isn't," I said, thinking about the extra prime steaks I'd bought on sale at Larry's last year, then ruined by leaving them in my freezer for too long. "Takes a good three months or more in the freezer to get that."

"Even less if you don't wrap things right," said Tanaka.

"This just gets weirder and weirder, man. Any other surprises about our boy?"

"Couple things."

"Such as?" I asked, bending down to examine the severed head more closely, going almost nose to nose with it, the sickly-sweet smell of death doing its best to push me away. The man's eyes were extremely bloodshot, but that was to be expected if he'd been frozen, all those tiny capillaries bursting as they expanded.

"He's got a deviated septum, Matt."

"Coke-head, huh?"

"Major coke-head. M.E. caught it on the preliminary; said he'd never seen one so bad. He figured the guy could hardly function the way it was."

"Tough," I said, straightening up and backing off a few feet, barely able to take the smell much longer. "Whoever lopped off his head probably did him a favor."

"Did us a favor, too," said Tanaka. "Especially considering what we found with him in the locker."

"What was that?" I asked.

"A big gym-bag stuffed full of meth and powdered coke."

"No shit?"

"A whole lot of each," Tanaka told me. "Maybe worth half a mil or more if it got stepped on hard enough. Good it never hit the street. Safe bet that's why he was killed – same for Rivers – major drug action."

"I don't know, Dale. I think there's more going on here than just drug action."

"Why do you say that? You know something I don't?"

I was about to show him the personnel roster that got delivered to my houseboat, when Doctor Peterson interrupted.

"This man was strangled," he called from the other end of the room, still working over the young girl's corpse. "That's the official cause of death for what it's worth. Look closely at what's left of his neck," he added. "Those are ligature marks just above his Adam's apple. The man was dead before his head was cut off."

"You sure you don't recognize him?" Tanaka asked me.

"Like I already told you: No! I don't recognize the guy." I turned towards the M.E., my knees suddenly feeling a little weak, and asked, "Where's the rest of the body? You haven't had any headless corpses turn up, have you?"

"Nary a one," he answered, without looking up from what he was doing. "We've had exactly five "John Does" through here in the last few months and all of them managed to hang onto their heads."

"Damn."

"Hey, Matt," said Tanaka, putting a gentle hand on my shoulder. "I didn't mean to press you, buddy, but I'm already getting heat from up top on this one. That new crime reporter from the Post Intelligencer is a total pit bull. A body turning up on Hendrix's grave is sure to sell newspapers. Not just here in Seattle, either. Whether it means anything or not, it's just the kind of hook that's already getting her by-line picked up by the major wire services."

"Screw 'em."

"Easy for you to say. You're not in the spotlight..." He paused. "Yet," he added, emphasizing the obvious implication.

I heard what he was telling me, but I was distracted by the sight of the head and who it reminded me of.

Ashcroft: fucking blown-to-shit cherry that hadn't lasted a week...

"Of course, she hasn't dug up any of the details so far," Tanaka was saying. *P.F.C. James Alan Ashcroft, nineteen, from Albuquerque, New Mexico...*

"But you know how she busted our balls on those Belltown murders last month."

Out on point instead of me for once...

"Shit, man, are you listening to me? We've got "20/20," "Hard Copy," and a couple other of those so-called T.V. news journal shows already nosing around to do a spot on it. This is becoming high-profile way before it ought to."

I'm slogging along, just behind Sgt. Rivers. I'm glad Ashcroft's got the point.

It's nice to have some company around me for a change, even if it is Rivers. Hard to be relaxed on patrol, but I'm a lot closer to it than usual. I listen to the jungle-buzz, that constant hum of insects and birds and whatever else that's always around us, and find it almost enjoyable and kind of soothing for once. As long as the jungle's making its normal noises, it's usually halfway safe...

"The new Chief is real displeased, Matt. He might bring the D. E. A. into this. Won't be good if he does."

All of a sudden, the jungle's quiet... Not a fucking sound... Totally still and silent...

"He told my Captain to nip it in the bud, or else. He doesn't want the press all over him."

We freeze. Stupid Ashcroft just keeps tramping ahead; hasn't got a clue..."If they get the Feds involved, we'll lose a lot of control."

In come the mortars! Thump! Ka-whump! We hit the dirt – the motherfuckers just pound us!

"Matt?"

I'm screaming and crying and shooting... So's everybody else... We open up with everything we've got! The ground shakes and shudders from the incoming mortar rounds. Dirt, trees, leaves and vines blowing up and swirling around like mini-tornados as we blindly sweep the jungle in front of us with suppressing fire. Our M-16's chattering through clip after clip and our M-60 machine-gun just cutting the shit out of things with its heavier caliber ammo.

"Look at me, buddy..." said Tanaka. "Hey, Matt, it's just some drug dealer's head, that's all. Right?"

"What's going on with him?"

"He'll be O.K., Doc."

The barrage stops as suddenly as it began. We're still freaked, and continue shooting until Sergeant Rivers shouts to cease fire. Then it's totally quiet again. There's no attack, no return fire. Probably just another damned hit and run. I'm thanking God, even though I never go to church. Can't believe it -- looks like most of the mortar rounds fell short. Can't tell if anybody's wounded, but nobody's crying out or calling for a medic. We're all spread out through the bush, staying low, holding our positions. Rivers has us sound off; gets a "Yo," back in answer to each of our names. All except Ashcroft.

Rivers orders Smitty and I to recon up front. We move out slow and at the ready. I can't see anything but shell holes and debris as we work our way forward towards Ashcroft's last position. I call his name, but I'm sure he's blown to shit because most of the mortar rounds fell where he was up on point. I don't want to see it...

"Here!" calls Smitty, just off to my right. I watch as he steps over a few

more feet, then kneels beside a tangle of vegetation next to a large shell hole. Then I see it... All mixed into the mess of vines and broad leaves is what's left of Ashcroft's body, one leg sticking out stiff and straight, the other bent and broken like a chicken's wishbone after a Sunday dinner.

"Man..." says Smitty, working to get him uncovered. "He's done... His guts are hanging out... Christ, he's got no head... Where's his head?"

"There's his helmet," I say, spotting it directly in front of me, about fifty feet away. I move up to check it out. I don't want to be doing this... I start to feel sick the closer I get to it. If his helmet's up here, his head might be, too. I've never seen a person's severed head... I don't want to...

Nearing the helmet, I see that it's resting top up, right on the lip of a shell crater. I don't see Ashcroft's head anywhere, and I'm glad. But it might be down in the bottom of the hole where I can't see it. Fucking-A, I don't want to look, but I've got to do it. I step up to the edge, and the dirt crumbles next to the helmet, and it rolls into the three-foot-deep crater and... Jesus... His head's still in the helmet! He's staring back at me with huge dead blue eyes... Got his chin-strap pulled down tight... Fucking fool! Rivers told me never to use the chin-strap! You don't ever strap it down, you let it hang loose on the sides whether your helmet jiggles around or not... Rivers told you like he told me, you dufus cherry. If you strap it down and get caught by a big enough blast, the force of the concussion can rip your fucking head clean off...

Jesus... Ashcroft's face is all grayish-pink... This smoky, oily color from the flash of the blast... Like a rare steak that flamed up on the B.B.Q. and you pulled it off the grill just before it totally burned... I can't take my eyes off of him...

"...Jesus..."

"Matt! Matt!" Tanaka's shaking me. The terrible face is still there. But it's not Ashcroft. It's the head here in the Morgue.

"I gotta get out of here." I push Tanaka away and head for the exit quick as my wobbly knees will let me.

"He seems pretty shook up," I hear the M.E. say behind me. "I don't know why – he's seen a lot worse things around this place than that man's head."

Chapter Four

I leaned against the side of the building. The fresh air felt good. It came in a gentle breeze blowing off the waterfront just a few blocks away and felt wonderfully cool as it brushed against my sweaty face. Even all the pedestrians bustling past me on the sidewalk felt good. Normally, I hated crowds of any kind. But these people belonged to the real world; they were out for a latte or shopping or just out seeing the sights, maybe taking a break from work, happily off to catch a movie or a thousand other things. Whatever they were up to, they belonged to the here and now, not some half-assed war thirty years ago that never should have happened.

"You doing better now, Matt?" asked Tanaka, coming up as I lit a smoke.

"Yeah."

"You sure? I haven't seen you act like that for a while. Way you jammed out of there, I thought maybe we were in for a repeat of last year after that bad business in Little Saigon."

"I'm fine," I told him. "And don't keep bringing that crap up. I went to the V.A. Hospital, like you were after me to do, and they took care of things. End of story."

"You only stayed a week."

"That's all I needed. I've been fixed up ever since."

"Yeah? What do you call what just happened?"

"A passing thing. Nothing to dwell on. A brief bad memory, O.K.?"

"Whatever you say."

"Listen," I said, flipping my cigarette towards the street so hard that it bounced off a shiny black BMW parked at the curb and left a little gray mark just under the front door handle. "You want to hear why I don't think this is only about drugs?"

"You're good at changing the subject, aren't you?" he said, with a small laugh. "O.K... Why?"

I paused and took a deep breath, pissed that I'd freaked out, but even more pissed that I'd lost it in front of Tanaka and the M.E. At length, I said, "Somebody stuck another copy of the personnel roster on my door."

"No shit?"

"Yeah."

"You see who did it?"

"No," I told him. "But my name's crossed off on this list. Counting that and Rivers' murder, I'd say somebody's probably targeting the members of my old unit. I need to find the bastard before anything else goes down."

"Man," said Tanaka, "if this turns into a serial murder case, I think the Chief is going to come unglued."

"Don't worry – I'll do my best to stay alive."

"Why's he after your old platoon? What's the motive?"

"All I can think of is some kind of revenge."

"For what?"

"Don't know."

"Well, you better start thinking, buddy. I know you did some things in Nam you're not proud of. You've never said what exactly, but maybe it has something to do with this."

"I don't see how."

"No?" He looked straight into my eyes and studied me for a few moments. When he saw that I wasn't volunteering anything, he said, "Fine. Don't talk about it. Damned war shit just eats you up all the time, but you won't ever talk about it. As it stands right now, there's a good chance this might relate to something you were involved in over there. Don't shine me on with this, "I don't see how" crap. You've got to deal with it at least for this case. Hell, I can imagine a million possibilities right off the top of my head."

"Such as?"

"You're not the easiest guy in the world to get along with. You've obviously rubbed someone the wrong way. Maybe it was somebody in your old unit itself. Maybe it's somebody with a long-standing case-of-the-ass at you, like that Corporal you told me about, the one who took over from Rivers when he left."

"Yeah, that's a possibility," I said, lighting up another smoke and watching all the people going to and fro, up and down the street, envying them for their seemingly ordinary lives, probably not having to deal with anything more troubling than what was for lunch or dinner, or whether or not the boss would give them a raise, or a thousand other mundane things. "But like you said, Dale, there's a million possibilities. For all we know, it might not have anything to do with the war at all. Could be it's some wacko whose beloved pet cat I ran down on a dark night and never even felt the bump. Stranger things have happened."

"Bullshit and you know it."

I smiled. "My point is," I told him, "that I'm not going to get all shook up over this until we develop some kind of concrete leads. All we'll do with a million possibilities at this point is probably run in circles and spin our wheels."

He nodded and said, "Just don't hold out on me, Matt, O.K.? You gotta keep me in the loop with this, that's all I meant. You don't win many popularity contests around the department. Pressure's on. Shit hits the fan and I get bumped off the case, you'll be all alone in the crapper."

• • •

Rachel had called me saying she had some news and wanted to meet. I'd faxed her the full platoon list, so I was definitely up for it. We met for coffee at one of her favorite places: Dilettante Chocolates on Capitol Hill. I think she liked the rich pastries that they served much better than their coffee. She was always snacking on one when we met, me usually running a little late like today.

I got a cup of coffee and wove my way through the crowded tables. I always got a kick out of the Dilettante, it attracted all types, like the Capitol Hill area itself, located as it was on Broadway Avenue, the neighborhood's two-mile long, main drag. When I was a young man, in the late 60's and early 70's, Broadway always buzzed with a busy, eclectic mix of people: blacks and whites of all ages, hippies and other long-hairs, assorted panhandlers, students from the nearby community college, straights, gays, small-time dope dealers, blue collar types and businessmen in suits and ties. It was no different today, except that the hippies had been replaced by Gen-X'ers and other grungers. The businessmen included a lot more businesswomen, half of whom, being dot. com. sorts, eschewed traditional business garb. The drug action had now moved to the south end of Broadway, where it centered around upper Pike and Pine Streets. Other than that, Capitol Hill had really changed very little from my Peace & Love era, save for having higher rents and many more upscale eateries and shops, like the Dilettante. Painted a rich chocolate brown on the inside, it was elegant but comfortable, and, like the famous chocolates they sold, exuded a rich and expensive patina, which made it just the sort of place you went to splurge and indulge yourself.

Today, however, I limited my indulgence to plain black drip-coffee and the opportunity to find out what Rachel had managed to dig up about my increasingly unsettling case.

"Matt," said Rachel, glancing up at me from her window seat, where she was spreading butter on top of an enormous croissant. "You should have one of these. They're fabulous."

"Don't you think it's redundant to put butter on a croissant?"

"Is that a crack about my weight, or what?"

I studied her a moment; liked the long print skirt she was wearing, as well as her light maroon jacket, kind of a raw silk material, but rather shiny and iridescent, quite reminiscent of the old Sharkskin that had been popular way back. It suited her. I liked Rachel. More importantly, I also trusted her. I had learned to not entirely trust most people over the years. My cop friend Dale Tanaka, my father, and Rachel Stern were about the only folks who had ever gained my complete trust. She had never done me wrong. But she could be a bit sensitive at times, especially about her tendency to put on the pounds. So, you had to watch how you phrased things in that regard. Beyond that, however, the simple fact was that she was really good people, had her head and her heart, not to mention her curves, all in the right places.

"You look great," I told her, taking a seat. "How's your case going?"

"Everyone seems to be suffering from paranoia. If I start acting weird, and telling you I think my phone is tapped, will you take me to a shrink?"

"That's the last place I'd take you, Rachel." They could take psychiatry and shove it, as far as I was concerned.

"So where would you take me?"

I grinned. "Tahiti?"

She laughed, then pointed at my lone cup of coffee. "That all you're having?" she asked.

"Yeah," I told her, glancing out the plate-glass window at the sunny sidewalk and usual Broadway bustle. "Good cup of coffee's all I need to go with whatever good news you've got for me." I took a sip. It was hot and dark and strong. "Either that, or it'll help wash down any bad news."

"I have both. Let me give you the good news first," she said, poking a finger around her plate and picking up the last crumbs of her croissant. Finished, she pulled a small notebook out of her oversized, brown leather purse and flipped quickly through its pages to the place she wanted. "I got the most information on this guy, Luther Brown. It was pretty easy.

He's a public official down in Oakland, California. Plenty of news articles about him. The search engine homed in on Mr. Brown right off the bat."

"A public official? Him? You sure we're talking about the same guy?"

"Luther Marcus Brown. That's the name you gave me."

"Yeah, well, he started going by the nickname of "Magic" in Nam. Kept hearing about all the race riots back home, and turned radical. Wanted to join the Black Panthers and grew a big Afro. Then later, he said was going to join Elijah Mohammed's Nation of Islam, as soon as his tour of duty was up, and started calling himself Shabazz. We called him by both names. Didn't bother him."

"Whether he turned Panther or Black Muslim or not," Rachel said, "he's still plain old Luther Marcus Brown from everything I've got on him. He's been a City Councilman in Oakland for the past eight years. Co-chair of the local Republican committee. Pretty high up in the party. A prominent businessman, too. Articles say he's worth millions."

I shook my head, hardly believing my ears. "What business is he in?"

"Investment banking," she told me. "I ran across a bio. item that had been done on him a couple years ago in honor of his fiftieth birthday. Said he started off with a single bank in the inner city in the mid-70's. Offered high interest mortgages to minorities that the main banks wouldn't loan to because of red-lining and such. Did so well that he expanded big time, had a chain of twenty banks by the early 80's."

"From radical to Republican," I commented, sipping at my coffee. "I guess stranger things have happened. Is that the good news?"

"Pretty much," she said, quietly, hesitating for just a moment. "Oh, I did manage to find an address for Jack Rivers."

I felt my heart rate speed up a bit. "That's really good news," I said. "Where?"

"Local." She pulled a small notebook out of her purse. "Just south of the Seattle city limits in Burien."

"Gimmee it," I told her, taking out my pocket notebook and pen.

"13816 Ambaum Blvd. South," she said, as I scribbled it down, thinking that it wasn't the best of neighborhoods.

"Where'd you get this?" I asked. "I didn't have much time, but I did check the phone book and information. He wasn't listed."

"I submitted his name to a couple of the search engines I use in my work," she said. "The odd thing is that he doesn't have any work history or credit history. That's unusual."

"Yeah, it is. So," I queried. "What's the bad news?"

"Well, two of these guys are dead. You probably already know about Ashcroft, because he died in Vietnam."

"Yeah," I said quietly. "I was just thinking about him."

"And Henry Baker," she told me.

"What happened to him?"

"He died a few days ago. I got the information from a reunion site for your old platoon," said Rachel. "Apparently it was a suicide. He jumped off the roof of an office building in Milwaukee." She handed me a printout which contained some messages that had been posted about Henry on the website. "Did you know you could still be in touch with a lot of vets if you had a computer?"

I glanced at the printout – I already had the info I needed about Baker. I gave her comment about me getting a computer similar short shrift – she was a bulldog, never gave up trying to drag me into the computer age.

"This is great work, Rachel. Thanks." I took a last swig of my coffee, then asked, "Will you keep working on the other names?"

She nodded the affirmative.

"Let me pay you for the work you've done so far," I said, reaching for my wallet.

"Forget it," said Rachel, waving a hand. "You can return the favor by doing some work for me later."

"You got it. Anytime." I gave her a quick hug, then hurried out and immediately got on the phone to Milwaukee.

• • •

"This is Detective Jarvis," answered the Milwaukee cop, sounding all stuffed up, like he had a bad cold.

"My name's Rossiter," I told him. "Matt Rossiter. I'm a P.I. in Seattle, Washington."

"That where you're calling from? Seattle?"

"Yeah."

"What's a P.I. from way out there calling Milwaukee P.D. for?" he asked, sniffling a bit as he finished his question.

"I was told that you're the one handling the Hank Baker case, correct?"

"Who? Oh, yeah, the jumper," he said, then coughed twice, really loud and phlegmy. "Sorry... This cold's a bitch," he apologized. "So, you know something about the late Mr. Baker? What's your connection?"

"Served in Nam with him. Haven't seen him since, though," I added, qualifying my statement. "I've got a case out here that may be linked to his death."

"That right?" he asked, starting to cough again, but sounding intrigued. "How so?"

I briefly told him about Sgt. Rivers and the platoon list that had been found on his body – asked if Baker had left a suicide note or anything.

"That's an interesting coincidence, Mr. Rossiter. We did find a note on this Baker guy. It was pinned to his sports coat. Wasn't addressed to you, however. Wasn't addressed to anybody, as far as we can tell."

"What did it say?" I asked.

"Damned cryptic," said the detective. "Wait a minute, I've got the exact words in my notes... ...wherever the hell they are..." There was a short pause. I heard him fumbling around, then he coughed again, dropped the receiver, said, "damn," then picked it back up and said, "sorry about that...can't find the note. Anyway, it was something about him being apologetic and…uh…kissing the sky, that's it."

I was quiet a moment, the old Hendrix tune immediately playing in my head, as my gut felt more and more hollow. At length, I said, "That note *is* addressed to me, detective."

Chapter Five

I kept Tanaka in the loop, like he'd asked me. Told him the story about Baker's death in Milwaukee and left him to handle the long-distance preliminaries with Detective Jarvis, considering it was an official police investigation. While he gathered background from Milwaukee, I said I had another matter to attend to and, of course, I'd make myself available for the inevitable conference-call with Jarvis. I'd covered all the bases with him during our initial conversation, and there was no point in my wasting time while he and Tanaka re-hashed everything. I'd be around when they needed me. Hightailing it out to Rivers' Burien address was the only little part of the loop that I chose to leave Tanaka out of in the meantime. No point in splicing him into it when I didn't have anything concrete to give him.

Ambaum Blvd. South was a busy drag that knifed through several bad neighborhoods. Like a lot of the south end, there were some nice, even upscale areas, but they were few and far between, and in order to get to them, you had to go through a checkerboard of seedy districts, high-crime areas and/or ubiquitous public housing projects. It was a part of town that I cared little for and frequented even less. Unless I had to.

The address Rachel had given me turned out to be a fairly large but unkempt Cape Cod that was sandwiched in between "Fast Eddie's" convenience store and a small video rental place that had both its front windows broken and half covered with plywood, a "Closed -- Gone Out Of Business" sign nailed up over its main entrance. The house had a rusty chain link fence around the front yard, which had been mown fairly recently, but other than that, there was nothing much to distinguish it from the rest of its shabby neighbors, except for the shiny black Mercedes sedan that was parked halfway up its long, cracked concrete driveway.

To say the expensive car seemed out of place would have been a major understatement. An "E-Series." Big as they got. New, too, from the looks of it.

I pulled into the driveway and parked behind it. Walking past the Mercedes toward the house's front door, I noticed that while the fancy ride was washed and waxed to perfection, its interior was full of clutter. Front and back seat both. The soft black leather seats were strewn with half a dozen or more Happy Meal boxes from McDonald's, complete with a few empty French Fry bags.

Must have kids, I thought, as I neared the front steps and heard loud music coming from inside the house. The volume was really cranked; I could hear the tune playing clear as a bell: Hendrix's *Castles Made of Sand* – one of Jimi's slower pieces, sad and wistful. The song finished as I got to the top of the stairs, then immediately began to replay.

I rang the doorbell but got no response, which wasn't surprising considering how loud the music was. Hoping to catch somebody's attention, I leaned out over the porch's low railing and managed to get a look inside through the house's picture window, where I saw a tall woman dancing by herself in the middle of the living-room. As I watched, she took a slug from a half-empty bottle of Jack Daniels that stood on the coffee table in front of the sofa, then went back to her solitary dancing. In her late twenties, at most, she was thin and pretty hot -- had angular but attractive features and long blonde hair with a slight wave that flipped and twirled with each of the sensuous dance steps she made. She was graceful, too, so smooth and effortless that I almost imagined she was dancing with a partner. Every now and then, she'd put her right hand out in front of her, then it would go up in the air and she'd twirl, as if the pretend partner was whirling her around the dance floor. But for all that, she didn't seem happy – had a mournful expression – looked like she'd been crying. Fair guess she was connected to Rivers in some way and had heard about his murder.

I knocked hard at the window and got her attention. She was startled seeing me peering in at her. I smiled as warm and non-threatening as I could, and motioned for her to come to the door. She gave me a hard look, then dabbed at her eyes with the back of her hands, and did as I requested.

The door opened about three inches – only as far as the heavy, inside chain-lock would allow.

"I already talked to you people," she said through the barely parted doorway, her voice low for a woman and less than friendly. "I don't know anything else. Just leave me alone."

"You must think I'm a cop," I said.

"What?"

"I'm not a cop," I told her, having to almost yell to be heard above the music.

"Who are you, then? What do you want?"

"I'm a private detective. I just want to talk to you."

"About what?"

"Jack Rivers."

"He's dead," she said, her voice quavering.

"I know. I'm working to find out who killed him."

"What do you care?"

"Jack and I were friends during the war. I thought maybe you could help me."

Silence, except for the blaring *Castles Made of Sand*, which now started to play again for the third time. Then she turned and slammed the door in my face.

"Wait a minute!" I said. "Hey!" I yelled, knocking at the door. The only response I got was the music being turned up even louder.

I looked through the window, saw her returned to her solitary dancing. I banged on the glass, finally got her attention. She stopped dancing, put her hands on her hips, and glared at me from the middle of the living-room. I motioned for her to come over to the window. She shook her head. I motioned again and smiled. She frowned. I kept smiling. At length, she strode up to the window.

"What?" she asked, loud enough that I could hear her plainly through the thick plate glass and blaring music.

"Rivers and I weren't friends," I yelled back at her. "We just served together in Vietnam."

"So?"

"Actually, we didn't like each other."

Her eyes softened slightly. "Yeah?"

"Truth be told, we hated each other's guts!" I exclaimed.

At that, she smiled. A nice smile. Then she nodded and beckoned me to come over to the door again. As I got there, it opened as far as the heavy chain on the other side would allow. She studied me through the opening. Seeming to approve of what she saw, she said, "I didn't think you looked like any of the creeps he hung out with. You two hated each other, huh? You and I have something in common, then."

"Sounds that way," I agreed. "You think I could ask you a few questions?"

"What's your name?"

"Matt," I said. "Matt Rossiter."

"I'm Sheri," she told me. "You like dancing?"

"I've done a little," I said.

She looked me up and down. "You're kind of handsome, Matt. You'll do just fine. Come in and dance with me. I'm a little lonely, and you can ask your questions."

I got the distinct feeling there wouldn't be any answers unless I took her imaginary partner's place. So, I nodded and said, "Sure."

The door opened and she pulled me inside before I could say another word. She didn't waste any time, started moving to the music the instant we got into the living-room. The place reeked of marijuana. I spotted a full lid of dope sitting in plain view on the round table in the dining-room. A fat half-smoked joint rested on the lip of a big glass ashtray beside the Mary Jane. More liquor, something I couldn't identify in a tall green bottle, stood next to the ashtray.

Man, the dope's familiar sweet/heavy smell instantly reminded me of my lost years after I got back from Nam. Sex, drugs & rock n' roll: easy to fall into, hard to climb out of, especially when most of the girls I met during that time tended to crank up the stereo, then offer me a joint and themselves, like you couldn't have one without the other. It was a real trip coming back from all the shit in Nam to such an overwhelming abundance of personal freedom and pleasure. So, I got lost in it. Laid back and kicked around with a bunch of fellow travelers, who were really going nowhere, but thought we were on the road to Nirvana. Even began to think we could change the world, like Crosby, Stills & Nash were always singing, when the hard facts were, we could barely change ourselves. Me in particular.

Yeah, the years from '69 to '72 were a whole lot like Rivers' old lady, who was presently wanting me to kick up my heels with her: I didn't know whether I was coming or going, and didn't much give a damn, either. This woman was a little older than the hippie chicks I went out with back then, but she was definitely foxy enough to tempt me. Almost foxy enough to make me forget I'd finally given up the dope and followed my dad's footsteps into the private detective business, where I had a bit of a chance to occasionally change some small corner of the world. – but she was nowhere near foxy enough to get me to take any of the marijuana that she was inevitably going to offer me at some point or another. While I still appreciated sex & rock 'n roll, I'd given up the drug part of the equation a long time ago. The look in her eyes told me that sex could easily be forthcoming; but I had a lot of questions for her. So, I just enjoyed the rock n' roll and kept quiet for the time being, and did my best to match her dancing, figuring that more answers might come my way if I let her hang loose.

Sheri seemed amused at my efforts. "Yeah, you move pretty good."

I kept dancing with her as *Castles Made of Sand* kept repeating. At least it was the kind of dancing I was used to – free-form, not any kind of formal steps. I was a bit distracted by trying to dance while simultaneously taking in my surroundings and wondering if we were alone in the house. It felt a little surreal, suddenly being drawn into dancing with this stoned-out woman whom I wanted to question. Even so, I kind of enjoyed myself. Not completely, though. I always had an edge about me. I'd learned the hard way, over the years, that bad things often happened as soon as I relaxed.

"You always invite complete strangers in to dance?" I asked.

"Only the ones who don't like Jack," she responded.

"Been a lot of those?"

"Not nearly enough," she said. "But you gotta keep dancing if you want me to talk about him."

I kept my feet in motion, saying, "He's not my favorite subject either."

"So why talk about him at all?"

"Well," I told her. "There's two ways to handle bad news. You can ignore it, in which case it might just come back and bite you in the ass. Or, you can meet it head on and deal with it. Even if that means it'll still try and bite you. You've always got a better chance facing it."

"There's another way to handle bad news," she said, undulating closer to me. "You just say fuck it," she said. "When he says he loves you, then leaves without a word, you just say fuck it. When a month goes by, then two, then three, and he doesn't come back, you really say fuck it." She stopped dancing and grabbed the Jack Daniels off the coffee table. After taking a long pull from it, she offered it to me. I obliged by taking an equally long slug myself. Then she had another for good measure, and set the bottle back on the table, saying, "Finally you realize, just fuck it! It's not important at all." She paused, her pretty face ugly for the first time. A moment later, she wiped off her scowl, and said, "Screw this Hendrix song. It was our song, Jack's and mine."

"He liked Hendrix, huh?" I asked, thinking it was about the only thing Rivers and I had in common.

"Loved Jimi," she told me. "Castles made of sand – that's life, he always said – that's what it's like, just castles made of sand…" She looked wistful for a second, then said, "I'm gonna put on a little B.B. King, and we can slow dance and relax. Don't you go anywhere," she added, crossing to the other side of the room and punching some numbers into the CD player.

"You haven't seen Rivers in three months?" I asked, as she returned and pressed herself close to me, her arms snug around my waist, her eyes and smile growing more than a little wicked before answering my question with one of her own.

"What are you doing tonight?" she asked, taking the lead and guiding me forward and back and side to side as B.B. King's 'The Thrill Is Gone' began to play. I wasn't much of a slow-dancer, but I didn't really have to be, the way she was controlling the action and rubbing herself all over me. She was hot, no question; layered blonde hair, almond shaped blue eyes, high cheekbones, full, almost pouty lips, a squarish chin with a sexy cleft in it, very firm breasts, and a narrow waist that flared perfectly into just the right hips. But I had other priorities at the moment. When I hesitated to answer her invite, she said, "I won't bite, you know. I'm a little drunk and stoned, yeah, but it's only some B.C. Bud. I don't do coke or heavy shit anymore. Jack took all that action with him when he left."

I stopped dancing. She continued on without my assistance. Sort of bumped and ground her way around me until she ended up behind me, her arms still tight about my waist, as I asked, "Rivers was into drugs?"

"I thought you said you knew him," she said, sliding in front of me again and taking hold of my hands. "Come-on, Matt Rossiter. There's a great dance at the Tukwila Tavern tonight. Live blues band, too. They're supposed to be smokin'. Pretty please? It's my birthday and I've been stood up."

"Happy birthday," I said. "Did Rivers just use, or was he dealing?"

She stopped dancing. "He gave me that Mercedes just before he left," she said, her blue eyes growing moist. "Now he's gone. Fuck it. At least it's paid for." She turned and walked towards the adjoining dining room, saying, "That fucking Billy. Damn him, anyway."

I followed her to the round oak dining table, where she picked what was left of her joint and fastened it into a small silver roach-clip. "Who's Billy?" I asked, as she lit up and took a deep hit off of it.

"I sure can pick 'em," she said, coughing once, then taking another big toke.

"He your new boyfriend?"

"Who knows, anymore?" She took yet another hit, then offered the joint to me, saying, "You want some? It's good shit."

"No thanks," I told her, pushing her hand away. "I don't do that anymore."

"Why not?" she asked, shoving it at me again.

"Don't," I said, swatting her hand away.

"Oh, come on." She tried again.

"Look! I don't like things shoved in my face," I said, grabbing her wrist firmly, and handing it and the dope back to her.

"I can see that," she said, rubbing her wrist as I let go of it. "You're a tough guy, aren't you? I like that, but lighten up. Have a drink with me, then." She picked up the green bottle, which I now recognized as that god-awful Schnapps called Jägermeister that had become so popular lately.

"No thanks," I said.

"Whatever," she told me. Then she shrugged, and chugged a fair amount straight from the bottle. "How about a beer?" she asked, when she was done. "I think Billy might have left some Miller in the refrigerator."

"Fine," I told her. As she headed for the kitchen, I said, "I'm interested in this Billy. Is he your boyfriend?" I asked again.

"Who cares?" she yelled. I heard the refrigerator door open, then slam shut. She returned with a long-necked bottle of Miller High-Life, twisting the cap off for me as she approached. "Why should you care if I don't care?" she asked, handing me the beer. "Hell, I don't even care that you're starting to sound like a cop."

"I'm not a cop. I'm private, like I told you," I said, taking a welcome swallow of the Miller. "Did this Billy know Rivers?"

"What, you're like Magnum P.I.?" she asked, sitting at the table and taking the last hit from what was left of the roach. "You're almost as handsome as he is," she said, leaning across the table towards me. "You know that?" she asked, her eyes going all dreamy and glazing over.

"If you say so," I said, wondering, despite what she'd told me, if she had anything else in her system besides just the Mary Jane. "Did Billy know Rivers?" I repeated.

"You gotta go dancing with me," she said, starting to nod off a little. "It's my birthday." She put both elbows on the table and propped her chin up between her palms. "Lots of guys want to go out with me, you know... I can have anybody I want..."

A loud buzzing sound suddenly went off, startling me. It stayed constant; came from across the room through the open doorway that led into the kitchen. "What the hell is that?" I asked, over the din of the music and the irritating new noise.

"That's just the oven timer," she said, lazily, still resting her chin in her hands. "You want to go turn that off for me? I'm a little too buzzed to get up right now." She laughed, then added, "Buzzed... That's funny... We're both buzzed, the oven and me."

"What's it for? You have something in the oven?" I asked, getting up and going into the kitchen, glad to turn the damned thing off.

"My birthday cake," she replied, turning around and looking at me through the doorway while I found the timer switch and got it shut off.

"Yeah, I can smell it, now," I told her.

"Take it out for me, and set it on the counter, huh?"

I found a pot-holder and took the cake out – chocolate from the looks of it. Then, I returned to my seat opposite her at the dining room table.

"Thanks," said Sheri. "Can't have your own birthday cake burn up in the oven – even if there isn't any party." She took another slug of Jägermeister, then said, "I wish you could frost them while they're still hot. I just love hot cake."

I'd gotten as far as I could being nice, and decided to change tactics. "Cut the crap and talk to me about Billy," I snapped. That got her attention. She frowned at my rude behavior, but also had a smile in her eyes, like I thought she would, from being ordered around. Same look of satisfaction that she'd had when I'd grabbed her wrist a little too hard. This girl liked the rough stuff. I didn't. Not when it came to women. But I'd do whatever it took to find out more about Rivers.

"You're packing, aren't you?" she asked.

"Yes, I am."

"I knew it. I could feel it when we were slow dancing," she said, her lips curling into a small smile. "Can I see it?"

I reached under my shirt and pulled the pistol out.

"You're dangerous."

"Yes, I am."

She smiled fully and lit a cigarette as I put the .45 back where it belonged. "So's Billy," she said, toying with her lighter, a big old-fashioned Zippo like my own. "Yeah, he knew Jack. They go way back."

"How far back?"

"Ten, twelve years. Something like that."

"How do they know each other?"

"Bikes."

"Bikes?"

"Like in motorcycles, you know?" she said, taking another guzzle of Jägermeister and blowing smoke through her nose as she swallowed the drink. "Choppers. Big old Harley Hogs," she added, taking another swig from the bottle. "That's how they met, anyway. They rode together."

"Were they in a gang together? The Desperados?"

"Yeah," she told me. "They were tight with other clubs, too. Even hung out with some of the independent ones."

From what I knew about bikers, they didn't mix much with rival gangs. Just being accepted, as an outsider, by one of the clubs was no mean feat. If Rivers and Billy were circulating freely between different clubs, they must have had something that each of the clubs needed.

"They ran drugs with the biker-gangs, didn't they?" I asked.

"Hey-hey! I don't get into that," she exclaimed, jumping like I'd just stuck her with a pin. "Jesus... You want to get me killed? Let's just talk about the dance tonight." She picked up the Zippo again, and began nervously clicking its chrome lid open and closed. It was loud and irritating. So, I reached out and took it away from her. That's when I noticed the engraving on the reverse side of it. That and the bas-relief shoulder-patch of the First Infantry Division. "Sgt. Daniel Rivers -- 2nd Squad, 1st Platoon, Company B -- Big Red One," read the engraving, below which was the insignia of my old division: a vertical arrow-shaped field of olive-drab, overlaid with a big red numeral "1."

"Yeah, that's Jack's lighter," she said, reading the recognition on my face. "He saved all sorts of old shit from the war," she continued, eagerly, seeming glad to change the subject from bikers and drugs. "I've still got all of it downstairs in the rec-room."

"Show me," I told her.

Chapter Six

As Sheri led the way into the basement, I decided to keep mum about the drug action for the time being. There would be plenty of time to delve back into it after she'd shown me Rivers' war memorabilia. Who knew; I might even find something in his souvenirs that would clue me in better on whatever the hell was going on.

"Here," she said, leading me into a large room that had been framed into the back half of the otherwise dank and concrete-floored old basement. She flicked on the light, and I saw that it was nicely appointed. Had thick, cream-colored wall-to-wall carpeting, mahogany paneled walls, and a long brown leather sofa that faced an enormous rear-projection big-screen T.V., complete with a fancy Bose surround-sound audio system.

But what really caught my eye, was on the other side of the room. A huge Big Red One Divisional Flag was stretched across the wall above an old-fashioned oak desk. Just below it was an American Flag and the old yellow and red South Vietnamese Flag. The flags were bracketed by two assault-rifles: an M-16 mounted on the wall to the right, and an AK-47 mounted to the left. Underneath the flags, were two things that drew my close attention. One of them was a shadow-box containing Rivers' various overseas campaign ribbons, including his combat infantry badge and a Bronze Star for valor. Beside it was an 8x10 photo of our entire squad.

God, that photo hit me like a ton of bricks. I remembered exactly when it had been taken – late September of 1968 – when I'd only been in-country a short while. There we all were, fucking fagged out, hang-dog and dirty, and just glad to be alive. Rivers had insisted on a photograph, just after we'd mopped up and burned that little village. He'd gotten some grunt from another squad to take our picture. I don't remember who, but I do remember the guy saying, "one-two-three, smile for the camera!" but there wasn't a smile in sight, just hollow eyes and filthy faces... All except Sgt. Rivers: there he was, larger than life, standing in the middle of us, crowded right in next to me, grinning like the evil fucking madman he was, his M-16 held high in the air with one hand, the other holding up his damned string of dried Viet Cong ears, three fresh ones recently added and still dripping blood...dripping that god-awful blood straight onto my shoulder...

"Sonofabitch..." I muttered and turned away.

"Hey, are you all right?" asked Sheri, coming over and putting her hand on my shoulder.

"No," I said, jerking away from her. "No. I'm not all right."

I was interrupted by the unmistakable grumble of a big Harley revving its engine. It roared loudly even though we were clear down in the basement. Quickly revved three more times before it abruptly shut off.

"Oh, shit!" she exclaimed. "That's Billy."

"I thought you said he'd stood you up."

"Does this crap to me all the time," she stammered, a bit frantic. "You gotta get out of here."

"Why?"

"Billy can have a bad temper."

"So, can I," I told her. "But, fine, I'll go. Can I take this photo with me?"

"Sure," she said. "Take anything you want. Just get out of here."

As I went up the basement steps, Sheri followed close behind. "Go out the back door, OK?"

"My car's out front," I told her. "Not out back."

"But— "

"Thanks for everything," I said, then went out the front door, and closed it behind me.

I expected trouble, but was surprised. Billy was inspecting my Firebird, obviously admiring it. I appraised him as he slowly walked around my car. Somewhere in his mid-thirties, he was a little shorter than my six feet, wore a black motorcycle jacket, with a 'Desperados' patch on the back, and was built trim and lean. He had a day or two's worth of bluish-black stubble on his face, high cheekbones with a strong chin, and was handsome in a rough sort of way. He wore a tightly wound red bandana as a headband, and his jet-black hair, cut short and spikey on top, had quite a shine to it. A long drooping moustache, with a triangular catfish grown just below his lower lip, completed his classic bad-boy look.

"Nice wheels, man," he told me, as I walked up to him. "'67 Firebird 400. Mean machine. Real fast. Don't see many of these around."

"Thanks. You've got a sweet ride yourself. "I gestured at the motorcycle he'd parked close to my car. Billy's chopper was all custom, lots of chrome, front and rear fenders removed, black teardrop gas tank, a long, raked front-fork, with an extra wide rear tire, and hi-rise handlebars. "Beautiful bike," I added.

"Thanks," he said. Then, the pleasantries over, he asked, "So who are you?"

"Matt Rossiter. I served with Jack in Nam."

"Yeah?"

"I'm a PI, now. I'm trying to find out who killed him."

"That right?" He studied me for a second. "Well good. Hope you do," Billy continued. "Jack and I go way back. Rode together a lot of years."

"Know anybody who might have done it?"

"Well..." He hesitated. "Not really. Anyway," he continued, "if you need some help, you know where to find me. We don't like our club members getting whacked. Right now, though, I've got to get inside. It's my old lady's birthday."

"Wish her a happy birthday for me," I said.

"I will."

We shook hands, and Billy went into the house. I got into my car and cranked up the Firebird's 500 horses. The quad exhausts growled, then settled into a low and throaty rumble, the kind that big cats make after they've brought down some game and eaten their fill. I'd gotten more information than I expected, especially the photo of my old unit, which I laid on the passenger seat for future reference.

I backed out of the driveway, then punched it. The posi-traction held the rear-end steady as I laid rubber and burned up the street. The wind in my hair felt good.

Chapter Seven

It didn't take long for my exhilaration to fade away. Happened shortly after I'd turned the engine off and come back to the car with my Dick's Deluxe, fries and chocolate shake. I hadn't been to Dick's Drive-In for a while and thought it would be a kick. It was a kick all right. Just about kicked my butt.

The place was crowded, as usual. Just as popular with the kids as it had been in my day. But whereas the big parking lot used to be jammed with hot rods and muscle-cars, today it was packed with Hondas, Acura's and the like, those foreign four and six-bangers that had come to dominate the roads these days. Which was fine. Times change. I could deal with that. But I wasn't ready to get caught in an unexpected time-warp.

Biting into my burger, I studied the photograph of Rivers and my old platoon, which was laying on the front passenger seat. I was listening to a tape in the eight-track: Hendrix's song, "Manic Depression." And that did it. Took me to the Twilight Zone. The music and the photo and Dick's all combined to just zone me out. I had sat in this very car, bought new with the money I saved in high-school, and had eaten my last burger right here at Dick's Drive-in, drunk on my ass in the midnight hour, before I went into the Army. I'd been playing some Hendrix back then, too – him singing about shooting his old lady down.

Only I was a little young to have an old lady. Didn't even have a girlfriend anymore. My steady, Mary Masterson, who I'd pinned in my Junior year, had chosen the night of the Senior Prom to break up with me. Tall, blonde, and a little wild, we'd danced the night away, then she told me how handsome I looked in my tuxedo and handed my Senior Pin back to me, and that was that.

Six months later, after Basic and Advanced Infantry Training, I was still alone. I'd gone out with other girls since joining the Army, but nobody ever tasted and smelled quite like Mary.

So now I'd become a man and was headed overseas to fight a "man's war." So, my old man had told me earlier that same evening. My dad, Jake. Tough bastard who I hardly ever saw because I lived with my aunt and he was always too busy working to spend much time with me. Jake Rossiter, ex-Marine, World War Two vet and former heavyweight boxer who I thought was the Second Coming of John Wayne and Robert Mitchum put together. He took me out for a special steak dinner that evening, even got his buddy, the bartender, to serve me some scotch when he told him that I was leaving for Vietnam soon.

After we had eaten, Jake gave me his advice, short and sweet as usual, "Be a man: fight fair, fight hard, but always fight to win," then apologized for not being able to see me off. He worked as a P.I. and had an all-night stake-out to pull. He walked away up the dark street and got into his deep blue '68 Buick Electra and drove off, me watching his tail-lights get smaller and smaller until they disappeared.

Man, the empty feeling in my heart and gut from that night is still burned into me as deep as all the shit from Nam...

And I'm suddenly in-country again: sweat hot, blown jungle, smoke and fire, smell of cordite and napalm, crump of mortars and Sgt. Rivers screaming, and all our faces covered with red dirt and fear, shooting until the clips run out and maybe we'll have to fix bayonets and maybe some of us like it that way.

Coleman's right beside me, burrowed into the dirt and freaked out. Heavy-set and muscular, you'd think he'd be tougher than he is. But he's just another FNG: "Fucking New Guy," and I wish I didn't have to rely on him. He got assigned to our squad right after me and I never let him forget it. Rode him harder than anyone else. It felt good to finally have somebody lower in the pecking order than myself. He was the "Fucking New Guy" now, not me. He'd be the one who'd have to walk point most of the time and hardly have anybody to talk to about how stinking scared he was, because we were all scared to be around another FNG. Damned dufus cherry who didn't know enough not to step on a mine, set off a booby-trap, or open his mouth when it should've been shut and draw fire when we were out on patrol.

Man, and here I am, stuck with Coleman covering my flank. Nobody could get you killed faster than another "Fucking New Guy." If he managed to stay alive for a few months, which most cherries didn't, then he'd be accepted as a veteran grunt and be able to take out all his rage and frustration on the next FNG to come along. Just like I did with him.

"Coleman! You dumb shit! Suck it up and lay down some fire!"

I felt sorry for him, even when I yelled at him, even when I told him that I didn't care whether he lived or died, even when I told him to stay the fuck away from me or he'd get us both killed. He never talked back, just stayed quiet most of the time and looked scarred and lonely like a little lost puppy, stuck out in the middle of six lanes of busy freeway.

"Get a fresh clip in your rifle you fuckhead!"

We're taking fire from the tree line, about fifty yards distant. Really heavy fire. Much more than a normal VC ambush. Feels like we've run into a whole company of NVA Regulars: machine-gun bullets kicking up so much red dirt around us that all we can do is keep our heads down and shoot blind, try to lay enough lead back into the trees that we can get the hell out of the open and pull back to the other side of the field that we've been caught in.

We're pinned down bad. Our radio-man's frantically calling for fire-support when Charlie's mortars begin firing. First couple rounds drop short, blow the shit out of nothing. Then the next few rounds go long, "Ka'whump! Ka'whump!" and shred the jungle behind us. They've got us bracketed, got the range; we're dead meat if we stay put. It's take our chances in the rain of bullets or get blown to pieces. Sgt. Rivers shouts to pull back, while he and Corporal Maloney try to lay down some covering fire for us.

We didi-mau out of there but quick. Stay low and zig-zag back towards the protection of the jungle. We can hear the mortars thumping behind us, and hear the "rat-tat-tat" of Rivers and Corporal Maloney emptying clip after clip trying to cover us, and smell the cordite and pray and scream as we run, the fucking terror so bad I can still taste the adrenalin that pumps my heart so fast I think it's going to blow right out of me.

Then nothing. Just this strange sudden blackness and wonderful silence. I'm floating through this beautiful void of quiet and calm. I feel totally relaxed and at peace. I must have died. I like being dead. It's so nice and easy. I should have gone and died sooner.

"Rossiter! Rossiter!"

Somebody's fucking with me.

"Come on, Rossiter. You're O.K. Wake up!"

There's this terrible burning ammonia smell in my nose. They're really fucking with me. I cough and see stars and push the hand holding the smelling salts away from me. I'm dead. I'm free. It's not fucking fair to bring me back to all this shit again.

Somebody sits me up and puts some tepid water down my throat from their green plastic canteen. The water tastes just as bad as the stinking green plastic smells. It's bullshit. It's all bullshit. "This is fucking bullshit," I say.

"You're all right," somebody tells me. "Bullet bounced off your helmet and

knocked you out cold, that's all."

"Cherry saved your ass, Rossiter," says Sgt. Rivers, his big ruddy face coming into focus above me. "How about that shit, huh? Coleman's not here a month and he drags your butt over a hundred yards, friggin' bullets and mortar rounds blowing up all around him. He wasn't still such a cherry, I'd recommend him for a Bronze Star."

As my head clears, I look around trying to spot Coleman, while the other guys go on about our artillery that evidently saved us.

"Sweetest fucking artillery strike I ever saw," says Private Owens, lighting up one of his fat White Owl cigars.

"Chewed their sorry asses but good," says somebody else.

"Must've had the whole friggin' fire-base ranged in on them," says "Magic," wiping his face with the ubiquitous olive-drab towel we all keep around our necks.

"Where's Coleman?" I ask, trying to stand up.

Owens gives me a hand, helps me to my feet. "He's over there," he says, pointing to a figure standing about forty feet away, his back to the rest of us, leaning heavily on his M-16 and gazing out over the pock-marked field where we almost bought it.

"Coleman!" barks Sgt. Rivers. "High-tail it over here! Rossiter's got something he wants to tell you."

Coleman hesitates, then slowly turns and trudges our way, dragging his rifle as he approaches.

"Tell him thanks, Rossiter," Rivers tells me. "Just look at that boy," he laughs. "Cherry's a fucking hero, but he still pissed his pants."

I step towards Coleman, my legs wobbly, my head still ringing, and offer him my hand. "Thanks, man," I tell him, trying to keep my eyes on his face, not the huge wet spot covering his crotch.

"Fuck you, Rossiter!" he explodes, smacking my hand away. "Fuck all of you!" he shouts, then turns away, his eyes full of tears.

"Let him go," Rivers tells me.

"Coleman---" I call, but Rivers cuts me off.

"What'd I tell you?" he snaps at me. Then he turns to the rest of the platoon, yelling, "O.K., all you sorry asses fall in! We've got some ground to cover back to base camp. On the double!"

I try to talk to Coleman a few more times as we make our way back, but he won't answer. Stays quiet the whole way. Won't talk to me at all. It goes on like that for almost a month. Then one day, he steps on an anti-personnel mine. He's lucky. Instead of killing him, it just shreds both of his feet. He's out of Nam for good.

I try to say goodbye as they load him into the Med-Evac copter. He doesn't say a word. They start to slide the door shut, and I apologize for having ridden him so much. He still won't say a word to me. The chopper revs up and takes off and that's the last I ever see of him.

But I hear about him two weeks later. Coleman killed himself. Committed suicide at the 106th Field Hospital in Yokohama, Japan when the docs finally told him they couldn't save his feet and would have to cut them off.

Fucking Coleman, anyway. I'm alive – he's dead.

Two days later, we get our next replacement. Another FNG. I go out of my way to show him the ropes. Help him however I can. Never stop thinking about Coleman.

Like now – sitting in the Dick's parking lot with a half-eaten Dick's Deluxe that's started to taste like shit – like what I did to Coleman. He's filling all my senses: I taste what I did to him, feel it, smell it, hear it, and worst of all, see what I did. Can't get his fucking dumbass face out of my mind. Not even my Wild Turkey can erase it – him smiling his dufus smile – big, happy-go-lucky kid who didn't stand a chance.

"Hey man, I don't mean to disturb you, but that's one really nice old Camaro you've got there."

The face leaning down at my car window pulled me back into real time. It belonged to a kid about the same age I was when I went to Nam. He had short brown hair, closely buzzed at the sides, with narrow side-burns and a short goatee to match.

"Say, are you O.K.?" he asked me, evidently noticing my sweaty condition and the fries I'd spilled in my lap while I was freaked out.

"I'm fine," I said, turning the tape-deck down as I cleaned up the fries and saw that they'd put some grease spots on my tan pants. "It's a Firebird," I corrected him. "Not a Camaro. They looked a lot alike in the late 60's."

"Yeah," he said, straightening up a bit and giving my Firebird 400 an admiring once over. "I thought it was 60's. What is it, a '68?"

"'67."

"Yeah," he said again, nodding his head appreciatively. "Big V-8, huh?"

"One of the biggest."

"Bet it really moves."

"It's a strong runner."

"Man, I've been thinking about getting one of these," he said. "They don't build 'em like this anymore, huh?"

"You got it," I said. "I bought it just before I got out of high school and went into the Army."

"You're kidding," he told me, with a shake of his head and a chuckle.

"No. Why should I be kidding?"

"Dude, this is almost spooky," he laughed. "What a trip. I just graduated in June and I'm going into the service, myself. The Marines. I leave for Basic Training next week."

I stared at him.

"Marines gave me a big enlistment bonus," he said. "I should have enough money to buy an old muscle-car like this when I get out of training."

"I'll be damned..." I said, the coincidence of meeting this kid making me feel a little strange.

"Hey, they could like start like an X-Files episode with something like this. That'd be cool, huh?"

I didn't respond. I felt a little weird and off-kilter again.

"What?" he asked, making an odd face. "Something wrong with what I said?"

"No," I told him. "Not really..." I put my burger aside and fired up the engine. "I gotta go."

"Damn, just listen that motor," he said, stepping back and smiling at the Firebird's low syncopated grumble. "Sounds like you've done some major work to it. What d'ya got in there, anyway?"

"Whole lot of memories," I said, putting it into gear. "Good luck, kid," I told him, hoping he'd have a better time of it in the service than I did.

"Thanks. Man, that's sweet. I'm going to get one of these babies for sure."

"Hang onto it if you do," I told him. Then I backed out and quickly left Dick's and the fresh-faced kid, soon to be a gyrene like my old man, far behind. As I sped up 45th, past my old high-school, and cranked up the Hendrix tape again. A new song began to play: "Castles in the Sand." Then I turned the picture of my platoon upside down so I wouldn't have to look at it. I leaned over, managed to roll down the passenger window, and stepped on the gas. Why the kid had gotten to me, I didn't know. Lots of kids still went into the service. But I felt light-headed and short of breath. I thought of how innocent I had been and how much had changed. Everything had changed and nothing had changed.

Chapter Eight

When I got back to the houseboat, I cracked open a new bottle of Wild Turkey, then sat at my kitchen table and studied the photo of my old platoon. Tried to come up with a name for each face. Nine people from the worst time of my life. Four of whom, I knew to be dead: Rivers, of course, Coleman, Ashcroft, and Baker who had gone off the rooftop in Milwaukee.

As I studied the picture, I was amazed at how young we were. At eighteen, I was the youngest in my platoon. But most of the other guys were only nineteen, and just a couple of them had reached the ripe old age of twenty. Only Rivers and Corporal Maloney were older, twenty-four and twenty-three respectively. Funny to think that we used to refer to them as the "old men."

I couldn't remember exactly when the picture had been taken. I figured it would come to me as I assigned names to the faces. Rivers and Corporal Maloney were easy, their features burned into my memory deeper than deep. Some of the others came back to me with almost equal ease: Ashcroft, Luther Brown, alias "Magic," Smitty, and Coleman, of course.

Well, a few didn't come back so easily. Actually, they kind of faded in and out as I looked at them. Weird how you can live so close to people for so long but not recall what some of them looked like. Probably because while we lived close, we didn't necessarily get close to each other. You make friends, they get killed, it's rough. So, we hardly made friends. We'd bullshit and carry on, yeah, but we always told ourselves if somebody bought it, that's just the way it goes. Shit happens.

But Coleman, he just keeps staring at me. He had that "Fucking New Guy" sunburn. Had it bad. His forearms and the lower half of his face, where it wasn't shaded by his helmet, were screaming cherry red. We had been told, when we first got in-country, not to roll up our sleeves, that we'd get the hell burned out of us from not being used to the tropical sun. But you'd just get too hot and roll up your sleeves anyway. And get burned so bad it blistered. Which is what Coleman had in the picture. Worst sunburn imaginable. I remember him whining about it and how he needed some First Aid, only a couple days after he joined us. The only First Aid he got from Rivers and me was being told what a dumb fuck he was and to shut up and live with it and by God learn to do what he was told from now on.

Poor bastard sure as hell didn't get any help from me while he was with us. Then he went and saved my life.

Damn… dirty sonofabitch...

My emotions suddenly threatened to overcome me. I could feel the tears welling up and wanting to come out. I hated it when that happened... Grabbed my bottle of whiskey and took it and my fucked-up feelings out onto the deck.

That's when I spotted it. A black video-cassette laying on top of my little white deck table. Somebody had been here while I was gone.

The bottle crashed and clattered at my feet as I instinctively reached for my pistol, ready for anything. But there wasn't a threat in sight. I left my pistol in its holster. I was alone. Just me and my adrenalin and the water gently lapping at the deck. And the video somebody had left on my table.

I approached it warily, my first inclination to be careful, it could be booby-trapped. But that was just more of that crazy crap left over in my head from the war. Whoever had delivered the video obviously wanted me to watch it. And the label on it left no doubt about it: 'Kissing the sky' it read.

I took it inside and plugged it into my VCR, afraid of what I might see.

The picture was dark and jumpy. After adjusting the tracking, the image of an empty rooftop came into view. A tight shot that framed the corner area of a high roof. It looked to have been taken from a distance of about thirty to forty feet away from the edge of the roof. The picture remained static, had no movement whatsoever, like the camcorder was mounted on a tripod rather than being hand-held. Everything was completely silent. I turned the volume up as far as it would go, but it stayed quiet, as if the video had been shot without sound.

The shot of the rooftop held steady for a few more seconds. Then the figure of a man entered the frame at the far left. He stopped at the edge of the roof, barely into view of the camera, which had been angled in such a way that he appeared only in profile. The man was a bit paunchy, and dressed in a light grey business suit. But couldn't see his face, because he was looking away off the rooftop. But there was no mistaking the gun at his back which had prodded him into position. I couldn't see who was holding the pistol, however. Only the leather-jacketed forearm of whoever held the silver automatic was in view of the camera.

Then the pistol waggled up and down. The man turned his head back towards the camera. Middle-aged and wearing a tightly trimmed grey beard, he spoke rapidly, as if pleading with the person held the gun. But I couldn't hear a word he was saying, because there was still no sound to go with the video.

The pistol jabbed sharply into his back and the man slowly and hesitantly turned and gazed off the roof again.

A sudden push and he was gone! Over the edge, face first, his arms reaching up as he fell, like he could somehow grab hold of the sky and save himself.

"Jesus..." I muttered, gulping down the last whiskey in my glass, riveted to the screen. But nothing else happened. The video ended exactly as it had begun. In total silence. Just the picture of the empty roof running for a few more seconds before everything went black.

"Jesus..." I repeated, pouring more whiskey and rewinding the video as fast as I could. Then I played it again. And again. And again.

Even when I finally stopped watching it, the video kept playing in my head. So, I went out onto my deck and tried to let it go. But I couldn't. I ended up blubbering like a baby... Why? Why? The damned senseless killing... all I could do was watch him die. Motherfucker...

I watched the video about a million more times. By the time I pulled it out of the VCR, I'd noted every detail in it, no matter how small.

Numb, I took myself to bed. For the time being, I couldn't do anything about this asshole that was after me and my old unit.

But there was another asshole I could do something about. Benny Luc. Bad actor if there ever was one. Terrorized Seattle's Little Saigon district for too long. I was set to testify at his trial in the morning, and needed to be in shape to do it.

Chapter Nine

I'd testified at more than a few trials over the years, but never looked forward to the process. Even when my testimony helped put away a few bad boys, it always set me up to be cross-examined by the defense, who typically dug up anything they could from my past in order to question my character. Since I was no kind of saint, they usually had some ammo to throw at me.

I parked and walked up the hill to the downtown courthouse. Once inside, I waited forever for the elevator, which wasn't anything new, as the busy courthouse elevators were usually so slow that you could just about grow a beard while waiting for them. When one finally arrived, I stepped back a pace as the doors opened, expecting the usual crowd to spill out. But it only contained a single occupant – none other than my ex-girlfriend, Jessica Ito, a rising star in the prosecutor's office, still sexy as hell, even in one of the severe business suits she favored for work, and one of the only women I think I was maybe in love with.

Fumbling with her purse, briefcase, and an armload of files, she didn't notice me at first.

"Hello, Jessica," I said, as she got everything balanced and stepped out of the elevator.

She paused and looked up at me. "Matt," she said. A trace of a smile appeared on her pretty face, but disappeared just as fast. The sad look in her deep brown eyes told the whole story: we'd had a big argument just after Christmas. She wanted to talk about it, but I didn't.

"You're looking good," I told her.

"Thanks," she said, as half a dozen people swarmed past us and got into the elevator.

I guess I was expecting her to say something else. When she didn't, I asked, "You ever buy that condo you showed me in Belltown?"

"I closed on it in February."

"Great. I'm happy for you. That was a nice, big place."

"Yes," she said, quietly. "Almost too big. It felt pretty empty for a while."

I didn't want to go there, and changed the subject. "So, how's the job?"

She gave me a look like she wanted to chide me for not buying into the guilt-trip. But instead, she said, "Same-o, same-o." Then she added, "What about you? I know you're here for the Benny Luc trial."

"Yeah. I'm due to testify in a few minutes. How's it going so far, do you know?"

"Not well, from what I hear," said Jessica. "Van Doren's prosecuting, and he's good, but so is the defense. The evidence is all circumstantial up to this point."

"It is in most cases," I said, the idea of a murdering bastard like Luc getting off just frigging inconceivable.

"Yes. But it normally takes a preponderance of it to convict. Van Doren's had three or four witnesses back out. They're too scared of Luc. So, it's a toss-up. Hopefully you'll have something concrete to add."

"I sure as hell do, and will," I said, even though I hadn't seen Luc actually pull the trigger.

Jessica glanced at her watch. "Well, I'm late for some depositions."

"Yeah, I've got to get going, too," I told her. "It was nice seeing you."

She locked eyes with me. "Was it?" Then, she strode down the hall, her heels clicking faster and faster, before I could even think about making a reply.

Jessica was much on my mind as I caught the next elevator up to the courtroom. The old attraction was still there. It had never left, really, just been put on hold. After we'd been seeing each other for a little more than a year, she'd wanted me to commit -- which was something I just don't do, or wasn't ready to do then, anyway. It all came to a head when, like a good prosecutor, she pressed me on the issue – pressed and kept pressing until I went out the door and didn't come back.

Even so, bumping into her again brought back a lot of good memories, too. As I got up to the courtroom, I found myself thinking about maybe giving her a call sometime.

Going into court, my eye was drawn immediately up front to the defendant's table. There, engaged in an animated conversation with his attorney, sat Benny Luc. He was dressed in a conservative grey suit, with a white shirt and maroon tie. If you hadn't seen him before, you'd think he was just another young professional, certainly not a cold-blooded killer who had led his gang robbing and extorting Seattle's Little Saigon neighborhood for the past several years. He'd even gotten rid of his trademark, long pony-tail in favor of a short haircut to complete his business-like appearance for court.

Didn't matter how he dressed, I knew Benny Luc for the charges that had finally brought him before the judge: the murder of his own accountant, and the man's wife and kid, after Dale Tanaka and I got too close to Luc's operation last year. We'd just gotten to his accountant's office building, when one of Luc's thug's started shooting at us. While Dale covered me, I dashed inside, only to find the accountant already shot in the head and Benny Luc just going out the office window and over the roof top. I managed to chase him down, but not before he ditched the murder weapon, which was never found.

Like he somehow sensed me thinking about him, Luc turned completely around at the defendant's table and flashed me a big grin as I took a seat at the back of the courtroom. I gave the little shit a bigger grin in return, even though I was now very concerned about the outcome of the trial.

I had truly been looking forward to this particular trial, however. If the defense came after me, fine: I saw what I saw, did what I did, and helped Tanaka bust up Benny Luc's protection racket and filthy human trafficking ring. So, a few hoods got killed in the process. Tough. They more than deserved it. Too bad we hadn't taken them all out – would've saved the expense of this trial. But of course, that wouldn't do. Everybody deserved their day in court. Even these dudes, and their gangbanger enforcers, who had terrorized half of Seattle's Asian community with their threats and shake-downs. They had murdered at will, once left a whole shipping container of their human cargo to die on the Seattle docks when we got too close, and even blew up a whole Vietnamese family at their restaurant in Little Saigon -- a father, young mother, and their six-month-old baby – in order to keep them quiet. That one really got to me. They never stood a chance. At least in Nam you could usually fight back.

Fuck my past and a few iffy things I might have done. I was eager to finally put all these bad boys away forever. A couple of Benny Luc's gang members had already gone down on separate charges – kidnapping, extortion, and conspiracy – but Benny, himself, was just coming to trial. Because none of his associates would flip on him, even when offered sweet deals from the prosecutor, Benny had skated so far. He'd spent the last few months in jail, still running his other rackets from the inside, so the story went, while the Fed's worked to build their case against him.

A lot of what they had was circumstantial at best. That didn't bother me too much, as I knew that most convictions were actually made on circumstantial evidence rather than on eye-witness accounts and such. What was upsetting, though, was that his high-priced attorney had filed a motion saying that his client was being denied his right to a speedy trial, and had forced Feds into court before they were completely ready. Van Doren, the Federal Prosecutor, had told me no big deal, they'd nail Benny for sure with my and Tanaka's testimony. But I could tell that he was worried. Van Doren was a big, blustery, Texas transplant who always exuded more confidence than a winning politician. But he kept looking away from me, now and then, when he told me that convicting Benny on first degree murder would still be a cake-walk. Besides, he added, they also had all the other charges against him.

That's when I knew that we could be in trouble. Van Doren always went for the gusto, would have normally cared little for the secondary charges if he was really sure of getting a conviction on the main count. So, I made the decision there and then to embellish my testimony if needed.

Benny Luc was the type who always had others do his dirty work. Kept him insulated from serious charges that could really put him away for a long time, like murder in this case. Since his people were ultra-loyal and/or terrified of him like everybody else he preyed upon, he'd never been convicted of a single damned thing, had slid by on every charge that had ever been brought against him. Everybody knew he was guilty as hell. But so, what? His obvious guilt, and always getting off, actually worked to Benny's benefit: who in their right mind would be a witness against this stone-cold killer who always gets exonerated and comes looking for you afterwards?

The gun battle that Tanaka and I had been in with him and his boys had been an aberration for Benny Luc. He'd taken part in a hit, himself, this time around: his own accountant, Lee Wong, and Wong's wife, down in Chinatown when the Feds had been squeezing Wong long and hard. The word we had was that Wong was hanging tough, wouldn't crack no matter what. But Benny wasn't taking any chances; uncharacteristically lost it and did the job on the accountant and his family in person.

Tanaka and I got there too late for the Wong's, but just in time to see Benny and three of his gang coming down the hall from his accountant's office. They still had their guns in their hands.

From that point, the short story is that they opened fire on us. I took out the punk in the lead, Tanaka wasted the second one, then

Benny ducked back into his accountant's office, while Tanaka chased the remaining hood down a stairwell and caught up to him in the street.

By the time I got into the office, Benny had gone out the window and up the fire escape to the roof. He seemed to know right where he was going – was halfway across the adjoining building's roof when I got up there after him.

"Why, Mr. Rossiter," he called out, when I drew a bead on him. "Don't shoot, I'm unarmed." Then he casually walked over and turned himself in. He was telling the truth, didn't have his pistol with him. What he did with it, I'll never know. The area was searched a thousand times, but his gun was never found. And it was his gun that must have been used on the accountant and his wife. Ballistics didn't match any of the weapons that his gang members had had on them. But we'd seen Benny and his boys exiting the murder scene, which was circumstantial without a ballistic match, sure, but was more than enough to hold them and get them charged with murder.

So, here I was today, about to testify, knowing that Van Doren, the prosecutor, was iffy about getting the murder conviction. No way was I taking a chance of Benny Luc walking on this one. Not after all he'd done. What I'd probably have to do was real simple. Tanaka had been absent fighting the other boy when I went into the office after Benny, so he couldn't say what I really saw. I had to make the case less circumstantial. The murder weapon being gone or not, all I needed to do was testify that I saw Benny Luc shoot the accountant and his wife. In this situation, I could live with that just fine.

Chapter Ten

I noticed an Asian man, in his late thirties or early forties, seated about five rows behind Benny Luc. He'd started looking my way when Luc and I exchanged our shit-eating grins. As our eyes met, the man smiled and nodded cordially at me, then turned back facing the front of the court.

Probably one of Luc's boys, I thought, although it would be strange for any of his gangsters to be dressed in a nice sport coat and tie like this guy was. Unless he was here to testify on behalf of his boss, that is, and wanted to present the best image to the jury. I'd have to keep my eye on him.

Just then, another Asian male, slid into the seat beside me. Young, dressed casually, and smelling strongly of garlic, he said, "This is for you," then handed me a small envelope.

"What's this?" I asked.

My answer was him getting up and leaving without another word.

Feeling a little edgy, I carefully opened the envelope and pulled out the note size piece of paper that it contained. It had a single sentence hand written on it in large, block style printing: *Testify and you die.*

I glanced up, saw Benny Luc staring at me again, this time with more of a leer than a grin. I held the note where he could see it and slowly crushed it in my hand. If he thought he could intimidate me like the poor bastard immigrants he preyed on, he had another thing coming. A whole lot more. From what Jessica had said about the way the trial was going, you'd think Luc would've played it smart knowing that I didn't really have that much to add with my testimony, not having witnessed him kill his accountant. My rendition of the events would only add to the circumstantial evidence against him. But Luc had reverted to his vicious usual form anyway, even though he'd silenced enough other witnesses to give himself more than a fair chance of getting acquitted.

I'd been thinking about that possibility of an acquittal ever since Jessica had warned me about it. No way could I let that happen. And

Luc's threatening note just clinched it. I now knew there was only one thing to do.

"Mr. Rossiter," Van Doren, the prosecutor, said, after I'd taken the oath to tell the truth, the whole truth, and nothing but the truth. "State your full name and occupation for the court, if you please."

"My name's Matt Rossiter," I said, feeling strangely calm, which was unusual when I was in the witness box. "I'm a licensed private investigator."

"And how long have you worked in this profession?"

"Since 1977," I told him. "Twenty-two years."

"That's a long time, isn't it?"

"Yes, it is."

Van Doren, his silver hair and friendly manner always making him look distinguished and likeable, looked toward the jury and repeated our conversation for their benefit. "Twenty-two years," he said, nodding his head and smiling. "Yes. A very long time as a trained professional in criminal matters." He turned back to me and asked, "Would you consider yourself an expert in this area, Mr. Rossiter?"

"Yes."

"Objection, your honor," said the defense counsel, Mr. Harvey Burns no less, expensive, slick, and very tricky – I'd run up against him before. "If the prosecution has a point, it would be nice if they'd get to it."

"I'm merely trying to establish the witness's credentials, your honor," said Van Doren.

"And trying to make a silk purse out of a sow's ear in the process," sniped Burns. "Rossiter's got a checkered past and everybody knows it."

"That'll be enough, Mr. Burns," said the judge, emphatically. "You'll get your turn on cross." The judge fixed his gaze on Van Doren. "You may continue, Mr. Van Doren, but the defense did have a point, so you get to *your* point sooner than later."

"Yes. Thank you, your honor," said Van Doren. "So, just for a quick recap before we move on, Mr. Rossiter," he said to me. "You're an expert in your field, that much we've established. I imagine, then, that you'd consider yourself an expert witness, as well – that is, a person infinitely more trained and skilled in observation than the average man or woman. Would that be a fair assumption?"

"You could say that. Yes."

"Indeed," said Van Doren, again looking at the jury as he continued. "We can *absolutely* say that. Mr. Rossiter is an expert witness." He glanced back at me. "So, in your own words, Mr. Rossiter, tell the ladies and gentlemen of the jury what you were doing on the afternoon of December 20, last year. Set the stage for us, if you will."

"All right," I told him. "On December 20, 1998, Lieutenant Dale Tanaka, Seattle P. D., and I got a tip about a case that we'd both been working on."

"That tip related to the defendant, Benny Luc, did it not," said Van Doren, pointing directly at Luc.

"Yes, it did," I agreed. "To make a long story short, we got word that Benny Luc was going to kill his accountant. He was going to do this in order to eliminate any paper trail and/or any possible testimony from the accountant about the illicit income from his criminal activities."

"Objection!" Burns fairly yelled, jumping to his feet. "That's just so much hearsay and innuendo. My client has never been convicted of a single illegal activity. Whatever this so-called tipster thought about motive regarding the allegations against Mr. Luc is only his unsubstantiated opinion and is completely without foundation. Therefore, I move that it be struck from the record."

"Your honor— "Van Doren started to say.

"I agree with defense counsel," said the judge. "The objection is sustained. But only as regards the second part of Mr. Rossiter's last statement." He looked toward the court reporter who had been busily recording the proceedings. "Let the record show that Lt. Tanaka and Mr. Rossiter received a tip alleging the defendant's involvement in a murder plot. The rest, however, relating to the defendant's possible motives for the alleged murder are ruled hearsay and ordered struck. The jury is to disregard that portion of Mr. Rossiter's testimony."

Burns sat down again. Looking smug, he whispered something in Luc's ear. Luc nodded his head and smiled, then stared straight at me, his eyes narrowing as his smile vanished.

"Alright, then," said Van Doren, acting like the judge's ruling hadn't phased him. "We'll just follow up on the tip for now. I imagine that's what Mr. Rossiter did," he told the jury. Then he asked me, "Did you act on the tip you received?"

"Yes. Lt. Tanaka and I responded to it right away."

"And where did that tip lead you?"

"To the office of Benny Luc's accountant," I answered, thinking that even with Burns's objections, everything was going pretty much the way that Van Doren had rehearsed my testimony.

"What happened when you got there?" Van Doren asked. "Did you and Lt. Tanaka try and prevent the murder of the defendant's accountant, Mr. John Lee?"

"Sure, we did. But we got shot at by Benny Luc's boys almost as soon as we got out of the car."

"I object," said Burns. "The witness has no way of knowing whether the men who shot at him were employees of Mr. Luc. They could have been anyone."

"Mr. Rossiter," the judge asked me, "do you have any proof that this fellow worked for the defendant."

"Not exactly. Tanaka covered me while I ran into the building to find the accountant. Then the guy got away from him. But it doesn't take a genius to figure out that— "

"Objection sustained," the judge said. "The jury is to disregard any relationship between this gunman and the defendant. You may continue, Mr. Rossiter."

Benny Luc laughed out loud at the judge's ruling.

"Counsel," the judge sternly warned Luc's attorney. "You tell your client if there are any more outbursts in my court, I'll hold him in contempt."

While Burns conferred quickly with Luc, Van Doren told me, "Go ahead, Mr. Rossiter, continue. You said that you went into the building to find Mr. Luc's accountant. Is that correct?"

"Yes."

"Did you find him?"

"Yes, I found him."

"Where was he?"

"In his office at his desk."

Van Doren paused. Then, in very serious tone, he asked, "And was anybody else present in the office when you got there?"

This was the part that Van Doren and I had gone over repeatedly before the trial – the part where I found Benny Luc just going out the window when I found the accountant dead at his desk. The office window was about fifteen feet from the desk and, while Van Doren certainly hadn't counseled me to lie, he made it clear that it wouldn't hurt a bit if I felt like placing Benny Luc a little closer to the desk when I came in and found the accountant shot to death. That could be as little as only few feet closer; maybe Luc not quite having gotten to the window, yet. According to Van Doren, a murder suspect's proximity to the victim could sometimes have a make or break effect on a jury in a circumstantial case without an eyewitness.

"Mr. Rossiter?" asked Van Doren, a trace of anxiety tingeing his voice, as I'd evidently waited too long with my answer while I'd been thinking.

"Yes," I said, loud and clear. "You bet there was somebody else in that office."

Van Doren nodded, and asked, "Who was that person, and what were they doing there?"

"It was the defendant, Benny Luc." I pointed him out for the jury. Then, keeping my voice firm and my tone even, I said, "I saw Benny Luc shoot his accountant point blank in the head."

Van Doren was speechless – looked like my lie had slapped him right across the face.

"That's fucking bullshit!" Benny Luc screamed, jumping up and slamming his fists into the defendant's table so hard that the thermos-pitcher of water on it fell over on its side. "That's a fucking lie and he knows it!"

"Order! Order in the court!" yelled the judge, banging his gavel repeatedly.

"Your honor!" hollered Burns above the din. "Your honor, this is not what Mr. Rossiter said at discovery, it's— "

"Mr. Rossiter!" bellowed Van Doren for all to hear. His expression was so serious it was almost a frown, but he had a little gleam in his eye as he drew the court's attention back to me – he knew damned well I'd lied, but was too good a prosecutor to let this opportunity pass by without reinforcing it for the jury. "Please repeat your last testimony for the court."

Staying calm and cool, I did just that: "Benny Luc murdered his accountant. I saw him shoot the man. Before I could stop him, he escaped out the office window, and I had to chase him down."

"Motherfucker!" Luc swore at the top of his lungs. He tried to lunge around the table, but his lawyer hung onto him. "I'm going to get you, Rossiter! I'll get you!"

"Bailiff!" shouted the judge, even as I was secretly hoping that Benny Luc would manage make it over to me. "Restrain that man!"

It took the bailiff and the court's gun-guard to get Luc under control. As they led him out, handcuffed and cursing, Van Doren sidled up close to me and quietly muttered, "Damn, Rossiter. Damn..."

The judge hammered his gavel again, then ordered, "I want both counsels at the bench. Now!"

Van Doren stepped over in front of the judge. Burns grabbed one of the files in front of him, and fairly ran up to the bench.

As they tried to hash out the situation, I grew tired of sitting, and stood up and stretched. I'd said what I had to – Benny Luc had tried to intimidate the wrong guy – I'd stuck it to him and was glad. And there was nobody to prove otherwise. Come what may, I'd stand by my testimony and hopefully see Luc go down for a long sentence.

The gavel banged again. "The court will take a short recess," said the judge. "Ten minutes. No longer."

"That include me, judge?" I asked.

"Yes. You may step down," he told me, "but only temporarily." Then he went back to his business trying to sort things out between the prosecution and defense.

I needed a smoke; wondered whether I had enough time to get outside and back. I'd just started for my original seat at the rear of the court, when I noticed the Asian guy who'd been sitting behind Luc on an intercept course toward me. He was coming pretty fast. I really didn't think Benny Luc would send somebody after me so soon, but I tensed out of reflex anyway as the man approached. He was taller than I thought from a distance – about my own height, six feet, with a narrow build. He smiled and looked friendly as he neared, but that didn't mean anything, especially with Luc's gang – he had plenty of boys who'd smile nice as your favorite aunt while they slipped a knife into your gut.

"Mr. Rossiter? Excuse me," he said, when he got up to me.

I stepped back slightly with my right foot, set myself, and kept an eye on his hands, which were out at his sides. "Yeah?" I said. "What can I do for you?"

"My name's Charlie Nguyen." He put out a hand for me to shake. "I wasn't sure if I'd have a chance to talk to you or not."

He didn't seem to be trying to pull anything, so I extended a hand. "What about?" I asked.

He clasped my hand with both of his, saying, "I saw you last May at the Little Saigon Awards Banquet when you were honored for all the good work you've done for our people. I'd hoped to meet you in person then, but got called away on a business matter."

"I see." It was time to end the handshake, but he kept hold of me as he continued.

"I'm honored to meet you, at last," he said, his dark eyes intense. "I have a number of investment interests in Little Saigon, and just want to personally thank you for helping Seattle's Vietnamese community, especially for putting an end to Benny Luc and his gang." He kept pumping and squeezing my hand as he spoke. "You deserve a medal for that alone."

"Well, it's not over, yet," I told him, trying again to take my hand back, but with no success.

"No, not yet," he said, his eyes seeming to bore right through me. "But it will be, soon," he added, giving one last shake, and finally letting go of me. "Everything finds its correct balance in the end," he said assuredly. "Of that, I am certain." He bowed slightly, giving me another warm smile.

"Hope so," I said, still concerned that Luc still had a chance of getting off, even with my testimony.

"The court is now in session," somebody announced. I looked around, saw that the Bailiff had returned – without Benny Luc, I noted.

"Well, I've got to get back to it," I told Nguyen. "Thanks for the good words. Maybe I'll run into you again, sometime."

"Indeed," he said. "I look forward to it."

"Mr. Rossiter," called the Bailiff. "Please re-take the witness stand."

I did as requested. Noted, as I did so, that Nguyen wasn't sticking around, was just going out the door of the courtroom.

"Be advised, you're still under oath, Mr. Rossiter," the Bailiff told me.

All was silent for a moment, then the judge glanced at his watch, and said, "The hour is getting late. The defendant is, unfortunately, absent. But I want to give the witness another chance to testify about what he saw before we adjourn for the day." He looked over at me, all steely-eyed, saying, "I want you to carefully consider your testimony, Mr. Rossiter. Are you prepared to do that?"

"Sure."

"Very well," the judge said. "Your witness, Mr. Van Doren."

The prosecutor approached the witness stand, his expression very serious. Burns, back at the defense table, craned his neck forward, and looked like he was champing at the bit.

"Mr. Rossiter," Van Doren said. "Tell the court, once again, what you saw when you went inside the office of Benny Luc's accountant."

"Same thing I said before: I saw Benny Luc shoot the man dead."

"I move for a mistrial, your honor!" yelled Burns.

"There'll be no mistrial on this, Mr. Burns," said the judge, raising his voice. "We went over this a minute ago at the bench. This is sworn testimony. It's up to you to refute it. However," he glanced pointedly at me, Van Doren, then back to Burns, "I *will* see you all in my chambers first thing in the morning. 7:30, sharp. Is that understood? Good. Court is adjourned."

Chapter Eleven

I felt better than I had in ages when I got back to the houseboat. I wasn't about to change my testimony, and Benny Luc was going down, the vicious little prick. At least something had gone right for a change.

But it only went right as far as that pleasant thought went. The photo of my old squad was still on the passenger seat, all those faces staring at me. I picked it up and stared back at them.

All of a sudden, another face was staring at me. It was Rachel, smiling at me through my rolled down driver's side window.

"Sorry Rachel," I told her, tossing the photo back on the seat beside me. "Didn't know you were there. I was in court today, testifying." She knew about the trial, knew it was a big case that took me back to Little Saigon.

"How's it going?" she asked.

I got out of the car. "Not good. I have to go back tomorrow to finish up my testimony. What's up?"

"I've got good news for you. I found another one of the guys in your squad."

"Oh, yeah," I said, more than liking that news. "Come on in. It's a beautiful day. We can have a drink on the deck."

Rachel followed me along the narrow dock to my houseboat. I dug the keys out of my pocket, as my resident duck family – a couple adults, and three little yellow ducklings, paddled over to us. They always expected a handout.

"Sorry guys," said Rachel, holding out her empty hands. As if they understood, they turned around and paddled back toward the front of my houseboat, maybe expecting better pickings once we'd gotten inside.

Rachel followed me in, but I stopped abruptly. My stereo was playing. Playing the Jimi Hendrix song: 'Let Me Stand Next to Your Fire.'

"Funny," I said. "I didn't leave the stereo on."

"It's a good tune," said Rachel.

"Yeah," I said, then headed for the kitchen. "What do you want to drink?"

"Got any coffee?"

"I'll put a pot on," I said, noticing that Rachel went over to the sliding door leading to my deck. Also, just past the deck, saw my duck family come into view. Smart little devils, I thought, as the sun on the water dazzled my eyes.

Rachel pulled at the slider, trying to get it open. It was old and sticky as ever.

"I thought you were going to fix this," she told me, tugging at the handle.

I started over to give her a hand. "Just lift up on it before you pull it."

She shook her head, evidently in response to my procrastination over getting the door repaired, then lifted up on the handle and it slid right open just as I'd told her.

"See?" I said, as she stepped through the open doorway. "Works like a—" "I cut myself short. Something glinted in the sun only one short step ahead of her on the deck: *a tripwire!* "Rachel!" I screamed, lunging toward her. Too late, her foot caught the wire an instant before I hit her like a linebacker, my momentum carrying us off the deck and into the lake.

Rachel came to the surface sputtering and wildly treading water, her eyes wide with shock and surprise. I put myself between her and the deck and hung on to her, shielding Rachel as best I could and wondering why we were still alive.

"Matt," she gasped, struggling against me. "Let go! What the hell are you doing? What's wrong with you?"

Then everything exploded. A huge *ka-rump sound,* familiar as a howitzer shell or a bomb going off: the insanely bright flash and shock-wave simultaneous, the concussion slamming into my back, the pressure pounding against my eardrums and blowing us further out into the water like gnats being swatted by some giant.

Debris raining down, I pulled Rachel under the surface with me for protection. When we came up for air, all was deathly silent, like the aftermath of a big storm or bloody battle. My deck was gone, along with the entire back half of my houseboat, countless pieces of which bobbed in the water around us – bits of roofing, chunks of jagged wood, one of my green plastic deck chairs, and tons of shit that was hardly recognizable.

Rachel was stunned. Semi-conscious, but out of it. I turned her onto her back in the water, slipped my left arm firmly under her shoulder and around her chest, then began to paddle, towing her quick as I could toward the nearest place to get out of the water, my neighbor's houseboat, some fifty feet distant.

All around, people had come out of their houseboats, wondering what had happened, some spotting us in the water and asking if we were all right, some jumping in to help us. I just kept going, intent on getting Rachel out.

By the time I reached the neighbor's small deck, and negotiated around the canoe they kept tied up there, two young guys I'd never met raced down the floating walkway and helped haul Rachel out of the water. She lay on her back, coughing and spitting water, but otherwise seemed to be in better shape than I imagined. I pulled myself up beside her, then noted that she had a trickle of blood coming out of her left ear.

"Call the fire department!" yelled the dark-haired kid who'd helped us. "That place is going up!"

I looked back at my houseboat – he was right – it had been engulfed in flames.

"Are you all right?" the other kid asked me.

"Yeah," I said, still staring across at my houseboat. Fuck it, I thought, it's only a houseboat – Rachel and I were O.K., that was all that mattered. I'd been through way worse.

Then I spotted something in the water about twenty feet from my flaming, ruined home: my duck family, floating on their sides, all dead as hell, their little, orange webbed-feet bobbing up and down listlessly.

I don't know why, but I started crying. Couldn't stop.

I held Rachel's hand as she lay on the neighbor's deck, while two EMT's worked on her.

"Ow!" she told them. "Stop it! That hurts!"

"Thank God you're alive, Rachel," I told her.

"No thanks to you! What the hell were you trying to do? Drown me?"

"Didn't you see it?" I asked her. "The tripwire on the deck? Someone set up a bomb – I don't know why it didn't go off right away. If it had, we'd both be dead." I looked toward the smoking remains of my houseboat. "I should have known it when I heard the Hendrix music playing."

"What?"

"There's a Hendrix connection with all of this."

"What about your houseboat," she asked, glancing over at the tower of smoke coming from it.

"It's gone. My ducks are dead, too." I turned away from her, glad she was coming around well, but not really wanting Rachel to see tears in my eyes.

The EMT's insisted that Rachel get to the hospital. They wanted me to go too, thought I might have a concussion. I told them I was fine, but wanted to ride with them and Rachel to the hospital, but they said I couldn't.

"Matt," she said, shivering under the blanket, as they put her on a gurney and wheeled her along the dock. "I don't want to go to the hospital. I don't need to."

"You have to," I told her, giving her hand a squeeze. "Just to get checked out, Rachel, make sure you're all right."

"What about you? You should go, too."

"I'm fine," I said. "Nothing wrong with me that a little Wild Turkey won't fix."

She looked like she was going to argue the point, but went into a real spate of the chills, even though it was over eighty degrees outside. I tucked the blanket snug under her chin and rubbed her hand. "I thought you were trying to drown me," she said, her voice almost a whisper.

"No. Not today, anyway," I told her.

She managed a small, teeth-chattering chuckle, then repeated herself, "Matt; your houseboat..."

"It's gone. Blown all to hell."

"Oh, Matt."

"Don't worry. I can always get another one. Can't replace you, though," I said.

As they loaded her into the aid car, the EMT nearest me said, "You sure you're all right, sir?"

"I've been blown up before," I told him. "You get used to it."

"Whatever," he said.

"You think she'll be OK?"

"Yes, I do. We'll be taking her to Harborview. They may want to keep her for observation."

"Fine," I told him, "I'll call and see how she's doing after I finish up. I have a feeling the cops are going to want to talk to me."

The Medic One drove off, and I began wondering if it was possible that Benny Luc could have been behind this. He'd vowed to get me earlier today. But a bomb triggered by a tripwire wasn't his style. Luc leaned to drive-by shootings and such, not anything as sophisticated as this. The tripwire was more a military style device like we and the Cong used to great effect in Nam. Also, there was the Hendrix song that had been playing on my tape deck when Rachel and I first got to my place. No way had I left it playing accidentally – I always check and make sure everything's off before I leave. Put Hendrix and the tripwire together, it pretty much eliminated Luc as a suspect in my opinion. Whoever had planted the bomb on my houseboat just about had to be the same person who'd been systematically killing my former squad members.

The delayed action of the tripwire bothered me a bit, though. Why the delay? Like I'd told Rachel, if it had triggered immediately, we would've been toast. In Nam, we'd sometimes use a delay hoping to catch not only the enemy point man, but both him and a few of the VC behind him after the wire was tripped. No point in that style in this case that I could see, however. Unless somebody was deliberately toying with me -- which I doubted. That left only a malfunction of the wire triggering mechanism, meaning that whoever set it up knew how to put the rig together, but wasn't necessarily all that experienced with it.

Whichever way it went, I wasn't any closer to finding out who was responsible for all the killings than I was when they first began. The sad truth was that some of my squad mates were dead, and the rest of us marked for death. And all I'd been doing was reacting. I needed to get on top of this but quick. I had to develop some solid leads and break this case.

But first, I had something very important to do.

I turned and started toward the long, floating dock that led out to the remains of my houseboat. I had a crowd of reporters to get by on my way. Bill Barkley, with Channel 5 News, shoved a mike at me and asked, "What can you tell us about this, Mr. Rossiter?"

"Nothing," I said, and kept walking.

The fireboat had finished hosing down the smoldering remnants of my houseboat when I got to the end of the dock. Wasn't much left of it, just part of the back wall on the north side, and most of the interior supporting beams that used to separate my bedroom from the living area. Everything else was either fallen in, or floating all over in the water. It hadn't sunk, at least – the big wooden floats that supported the houseboat were still intact. Three firemen were in the ruins poking around and putting out any last hot spots.

One of them saw me and made his way over to me on the dock. "You're the owner, right?" he asked.

"Yeah," I told him.

"You're not going to be able to go through what's left of your place until everything cools down," he told me. "But I did find one thing that I thought you'd want."

"What's that?"

He reached into the front pocket of his heavy fire coat, and pulled out an audio tape, still in its jacket. Handing it to me, he said, "I saw you had a huge collection. Afraid it's all melted except this one. Funny how some things survive without any damage at all."

As I took it from him, I saw which tape it was: *Are You Experienced?*, his first album from 1967. I could hardly believe it.

"Thanks," I said. "This means a lot to me."

"Don't mention it. I've got a big music collection myself. Well, good luck." With that, he went back to work.

Somebody tapped me on the shoulder. It was a police detective name Morgan, who was leading the investigation into the explosion. "Hope your friend's all right, Mr. Rossiter," he said. "You ready to talk with me?"

"In a minute," I told him. "I've got one last thing to do. It's important."

"Oh, yeah? What's that?"

His answer was me scanning the water all around my houseboat's side of the dock. It was getting toward dark, and a little hard to see, especially in the slight chop that had kicked up in the waning sunlight. But I was lucky, and one by one I found two little yellow and orange shapes, both bobbing near enough to the dock for me to gently fish out of the water. The third, I found had drifted partway under the narrow dock.

The three, little dead ducklings perfectly filled the palms of my cupped hands. When I found the mother duck, I'd bury her along with them in the community flower garden that our association kept shore side.

Chapter Twelve

It was after 9:00 PM when I finished up with the cops. The sun had almost set, the wind had died down, and the lake was calm and kind of glowing in the waning light. What was left of my houseboat was just a ragged, black shadow on the other side of the dock.

The cops wanted to know if I had any enemies. I told them of course I did. Couldn't be in my profession without making more than a few. As Benny Luc was the most obvious of the lot, they were especially interested in him. I did nothing to dissuade them, even though I'd pretty much eliminated Luc as a likely suspect. Anything that brought more heat on him was fine by me. And I'd turn up the heat even more when I talked to the judge in the morning.

Right now, I needed a drink. My whole life had just gone up in that explosion. Every material thing I'd ever cared about enough to save, anyway. As for the bucks it would take to replace my houseboat, I didn't care much about money – money was only worth what it could buy, and half of what it could buy wasn't worth much. No time to dwell on it, though. Before I chased down a little Wild Turkey, I had to see how Rachel was doing.

Without thinking, I started back up the dock to use the phone before realizing that it and most of my houseboat wasn't there anymore. I had to laugh – funny what can happen to your head when you've almost been blown to shit.

So, I needed to find a pay phone. I was pretty sure Pete's Market, across the way, had one.

They did, and I put in the call to Harborview. I was surprised to find out that they'd already treated and released her. Because of the privacy laws, they couldn't tell me anything about her condition, but it was a no-brainer to figure out that she was fine if they'd discharged her.

I went back over and sat in my car. I got my good friend, the Wild Turkey, out of the glove box and communed with him. Rachel was fine.

I was fine. Wild Turkey was fine. So why did I start shaking? Why was I feeling like I couldn't breathe?

My old squad members in the photo gave me the answer. Nam again. Always Nam. Sure, I should've expected this. Shit's bound to catch up with you. But you do what you've gotta do, then worry about it later.

If you don't deal with a trauma, it'll come back and bite you. The worse the trauma and the longer you wait to deal with it, the worse it'll get. That's what the idiot counselors at the V.A. kept telling me the short time I was there last year.

Easy to say. Easy to understand. Hard to do. Why did I do this PI work anyway? It could be high-test, could get physical, dangerous, even deadly. The only answer I could come up with was damn me anyway if I didn't just love it.

So, deal with it, I told myself. Get a grip. Relax. Take deep breaths. Drink more. You can't just sit here and fall apart.

I needed some help. And I knew just who could give it to me.

I cranked the engine over and headed toward Jessica Ito's condo in Belltown. She'd been on my mind ever since I'd bumped into her coming off that elevator at the courthouse. If Jessica couldn't help fix me, nobody could. Besides, I had nowhere else to spend the night.

Jessica's place was in one of the million new condos they'd built just north of the Public Market. Very expensive and upscale – far cry from the rundown area Belltown had been not that many years back. It still had many of the old early 1900's brick buildings, but they were turning into restaurants, classy bars, refurbished apartment buildings, and of course, new condominiums.

I rang the buzzer at the front entrance to her building.

"Yes? Who is it?" came Jessica's voice through the silver intercom.

"It's Matt. Can I come up?"

"Matt..." Her voice trailed off.

"Yeah."

"What are you doing here?"

"Can I come up?" I repeated.

After a long moment, the door buzzed, and I went in and took the elevator to her place on the third floor.

When I got down the hall, I found Jessica standing in the open doorway to her unit. She wore the short, silky, black nightgown and matching robe that I'd given her last Christmas. She was still so damned sexy and attractive that you didn't want to say anything, just let yourself be drawn up close to her and take it from there.

I started to do just that, but she put a hand against my chest and held me back.

"What," she told me, "do you think you can just waltz back into my life without a word?"

"I need you Jessica."

Her hand softened on my chest and I took her in my arms and swept her inside. She didn't resist, followed me almost as if we were dancing. She didn't say anything, and neither did I. Wasn't any need.

Her hands caressing my sides, we glided into the living room up near the wide, picture window with its view of Elliott Bay and the ever-busy Alaskan Way Viaduct. As we'd done so many times before, we undressed each other in front of an open window, the lights of a ferry coming into dock and the lights of the myriad cars going past on the nearby viaduct only adding to the excitement of the moment.

She smelled of lavender and Taboo. Felt soft, safe, and smooth.

Both naked, Jessica turned me around facing the window, pressed me up almost against the glass, and slowly began stroking me from behind. It was delicious. We'd hardly ever had sex at her place without performing this ritual. It was like I was hers and hers alone, and she wanted the whole world to see. If her exhibitionistic streak bothered me a bit the first time we'd ever made love, it quickly turned into an appreciation of her fetish when it came her turn to stand in front of the window: the cars going by would catch a small glimpse at best, maybe wonder at what they saw, maybe wonder what they were missing.

Jessica's bed was also near a large window facing the viaduct. We moved there to continue our lovemaking, a couple soft lights on, Jessica on top, which was what she liked best. When we were done, only then did she close the drapes.

The early morning sun woke me. Jessica was sleeping peacefully beside me. At least someone was peaceful. Me, I hadn't slept well at all. Never did, but I had even more on my mind than the usual bad dreams. I needed to call Rachel, make sure she was doing OK, then get busy trying to get a handle on all the shit that had been going down.

I slipped out of bed and quietly went into the living room, where I picked up the phone and called Rachel. When she picked right up, her voice strong as ever, I said, "Rachel. You sound good. Thank God you're OK."

"Matt. Thank God you're OK," she echoed me. "Where are you?"

"Ah, I went and stayed with Jessica Ito," I told her. "Didn't get a lot of sleep last night."

"Yeah, well neither did I." She paused a moment, then said, "Matt, someone returned my purse."

I couldn't believe it. I remembered she had her purse with her when we went into the lake, and thought it was probably gone forever. "That's great news, Rachel."

"Not really," she told me. "Whoever returned it broke into my house, plunked the purse down on my desk, and left a note saying you were lucky, but he would try again. The police took the note away to analyze it. A friend of yours, Dale Tanaka, was here. He wants you to call him."

"Will do." I was pissed about Rachel almost getting blown up along with my houseboat, but even more pissed that she continued to be in danger because of my shit.

"Someone's trying to kill you, Matt!"

"Yeah. Me and the members of my old squad. Didn't you say you'd found someone else from my unit?"

"I think so. I found a guy named William Riley."

"William Riley?"

"Went by the name of Boo," she told me.

"Oh, Boo! Sure, I know Boo."

She gave me his address.

"Really?" I said. "He's still in Bellingham?"

She read the address to me again.

"Wow! That's going to be a flashback to old times."

"What do you mean?" Rachel asked.

"That's where Boo was living when I got out of the Army. I went and stayed with him for a while."

"What's happening with your houseboat?" she asked.

"Going to have to start over," I said. "But I've got insurance."

"That's good, Matt."

"Thanks. I better split. I'm due in court in just a little bit."

I hung up, got dressed quick and quiet, didn't want to disturb Jessica, especially since I was in a hurry.

I got to the judge's chambers with only a minute to spare. Van Doren was there, same for Burns, Benny Luc's defense attorney. I expected to get reamed by Burns after my testimony yesterday. But the instant he opened his mouth, the judge told him to put a lid on it. That was good, I thought, a bad sign for Burns' trying to call for a mistrial.

The judge, though, surprised me. He just quietly asked me was if I was standing by my previous testimony.

"Yes, your honor," I said.

"So be it, Mr. Rossiter," he told me. "There will be no court this morning, gentlemen. I need time to consider the ramifications of Mr. Rossiter's testimony and the disposition of this case. You will all be notified when I complete my deliberations."

Then the judge ushered us out without another word.

Chapter Thirteen

I'd pissed a lot of people off. The defense attorney was pissed; the judge was pissed, even though he'd tried not to let it show too much; Jessica was pissed because she knew deep down inside that I'd lied; and Van Doren, the prosecutor, was only half-pissed – he'd be happy if my testimony stuck, but ready to lose it if anybody proved that I'd perjured myself, and his case went south. Guess that left me as the only person who was happy. Even though the judge had been tight-lipped, nobody could prove that I lied, so I was happy that Benny Luc would undoubtedly go down on the murder charge. I was also happy to be cruising north on I-5, listening to my Firebird purr. Most of all, I was happy I was on my way to see my old war buddy, Boo Riley, whom I hadn't seen in many years. Knowing Boo, he'd be Mr. Mellow and blow off my warning about whoever was killing our old squad members, while his total bad-ass side would tell me not to worry about him, he could take care of himself.

I couldn't believe it when Rachel told me she'd found Boo. The address she had for him blew my mind – it was the same address in the Fairhaven District in Bellingham where I'd stayed for three years after I'd gotten out of the Army so long ago. Too much! Boo and Smitty had been my only real friends in Nam. Boo saved my ass more than once, and I returned the favor more than once. He was the one who'd turned me on to dope being the best way to handle the stress and strain and horror of the war. Mary Jane, hash, blow, you name it, Boo had it or knew where to get it.

That's how he became known as Boo in our squad. Didn't matter what he was on – uppers, downers, psychedelics – he turned into one crazy motherfucker in a firefight. When we were on ambush duty, he didn't just shoot the Cong when we surprised them; he jumped out of cover like Jekyll and Hyde and always shouted, "Boo!" before shooting the shit out of them. He said it gave him the biggest rush to scare them good before wasting them.

His reputation for being a crazy bastard preceded him – not even Sgt. Rivers or Corporal Maloney fucked with him. Yeah, good old Boo. When we became tight, his nuttiness gave me a bit of shelter from Rivers, too, which was another reason to dig the guy. I hoped that he'd listen to me about the danger he was in, but I didn't really expect him to. Knowing him, he'd blow me off. But I had to try.

I would have called first rather than driving the 90 miles to Bellingham, but Boo never believed in phones, and Rachel naturally found no number for him. It was just par for the course with Boo -- he lived like a ghost where the authorities were concerned. The reason he had no phone was the same reason he gave me when I got out of the service and moved in with him: "Government's not getting hold of me again, dude," he told me over some good Acapulco Gold. "Screw 'em! They had me for two years. Never again. I don't exist. Hey, don't Bogart that joint!"

As I took the Fairhaven exit from the freeway, I thought about my years there. They were my lost years. I was just as lost as the time I spent in Nam. Drugs, sex, rock and roll, and more drugs, sex, and rock and roll. Easy to get lost in that rarified mix. On it went until I could hardly remember one day from the next, and didn't care, because the one thing that never got blotted out was Nam. Drugs made you live in the moment, which was good, but the past always came back to bite you. So, you toked up, dropped or snorted again -- and again and again and again -- and that's how it went feel mellow, feel like crap; feel mellow, feel like crap; and so on, until just before Nixon got forced out over Watergate, and I forced myself away from Bellingham and the drugs while there was still something left of me. That's when I joined up with Wild Turkey and never went back. Until now.

I hit the old town area of Fairhaven and watched the turn-of-the-century brick buildings roll by until I turned north and recognized Boo's house. It looked the same as it had twenty-five years ago – a big wood-framed house, painted bright green, on a wide, deep lot. It looked recently painted, but was the same color it had always been.

The front yard was made up almost entirely of wildflowers, with some tall flowers like dahlias, sunflowers, and others mixed in. With those, and its wide front porch, the place still looked like the cover of an old Crosby, Stills and Nash album.

I parked the car and walked up the wooden steps. I had to knock extra loud at the front door to be heard over the loud rock music coming from inside -- some Grateful Dead tune, though I couldn't say exactly which one.

The door finally opened. It was Boo himself, wearing a loud, rose-colored Hawaiian shirt, with white pants, and a pair of red flip-flops on his bare feet, complete with a pucka-shell ankle-bracelet above his right foot. He'd put on extra weight, like me – in his case, a little paunchy – but he still looked mostly the same, had a flowing mane of blond hair, done in a ponytail, with a big, grizzled moustache and beard, now flecked with gray. His piercing blue eyes were set above high cheekbones and a hawk-like nose. He was beyond tan, and looked like a hippie version of General George Armstrong Custer in a ponytail.

"Matt!" he fairly yelled. "Matt Rossiter, I'll be damned."

"Hey, Boo." I barely got his name out of my mouth, when he grabbed onto my arms and jerked me over the threshold.

We gave each other a bear hug inside the small foyer, then Boo stepped back and appraised me.

"Whoa, dude," he said, "you've gone all Eddie Bauer, huh? What's up with that?"

"I'm a private detective now," I told him, noticing the place still smelled the same: heavy aroma of Patchouli Oil, sandalwood, and marijuana. Much as I hated to admit it, my old nemesis, Mary Jane, was very inviting.

"No shit?" said Boo. "Private dick, you? No shit? You fought the law and the law won, huh?"

I smiled. "Yeah, you could say that." I took in the living room as I spoke. I felt like I'd just taken a time machine to back in the day -- it had hardly changed. Big, brown overstuffed sofa set against the wall facing the wood-framed front window, the molding of which was still stained a mahogany brown. The roughly stuccoed, interior walls were still painted the same too-bright yellow that made acid-trips so much more vivid. And that ultra-bright yellow was echoed in the sheets used to cover the windows instead of drapes: a light cotton cloth with a pastel yellow and brown pattern on it. I always thought the window coverings made the place look like more of a crash-pad than a house, but Boo loved it, wouldn't change it, said it reminded him of this east Indian babe he met in the Haight named Paisley -- "Her name was Navpreet, and she called herself Sweet, but everyone knew her as Paisley," he would say, laughing at his own joke and forever concluding with, "She had these ankle-brackets with tiny bells that jingled and jangled, and oooo-la-la, ain't this the best shit you ever smoked?" So, there was no arguing with him about changing the living room color or especially the paisley window coverings. I had to wonder, looking at them, if they could really be the same ones from back in the day.

"Place hasn't changed much," I told Boo.

"Like they say," he said, "if it ain't broke, don't fix it. And yeah, I saw you looking just now – and yes, these are the same sheets on the windows as when you were here last. So, sit down, share a jay, tell me why you waited so long to come see me again."

We sat down, him on the overstuffed sofa that had a sheet over it matching the window coverings, and me on the wide armchair set at an angle from the sofa.

"Doesn't seem like that long, actually," Boo continued, busy rolling a joint with his ever-present Zig Zag cigarette papers. "Then again, yeah, I guess it does. I thought, man, maybe you didn't like your old bro Boo anymore."

"Sorry about that, but you know why I left."

"Yeah," he said, "left to become Eddie Bauer Jr. you shit-bird. Seriously, though," he continued without missing a beat, "you got troubles, Matt? 'Course, you always had troubles, but I was there for you. Like now. Here," he lit the joint, took a hit, then stood and passed it over to me. "Fix your troubles better than before, 'cause this shit's twenty times stronger than it ever was. We used to have to blow through half a lid to get high sometimes, remember?"

"Somebody's killing our old squad members, Boo," I said.

"Yeah. I saw in the news that Rivers bought it," he said. "Good riddance. God rest his evil, fucked up soul, if he ever had one to begin with."

"Killed Baker, too," I told him. "Whoever's behind it has our names from one of our squad lists from Nam. They already tried to take me out."

"But they couldn't kill you, right? You here to warn me?"

"That's the gist of it."

"No worries, man. I'm hard to kill. You know that."

"This is serious, Boo. List this guy's got is from '68. There were only nine of us then. I've got another private detective trying to locate everybody. I know that Magic's in Oakland, but I haven't located Corporal Maloney or Smitty."

"Maloney," said Boo, almost spitting the name out. "Anybody else deserves to get wasted, it's that prick."

"Well, I still have to— "

"And Magic," Boo continued. "I haven't thought about him for years. He's from Oakland, right?"

"Yeah," I said. "But think about yourself, Boo. You need to take some precautions."

"Fuck it. I'm fine."

"Look, man, your name's on the list and— "

"Gimme that jay back if you're not going to smoke it." I handed it over, and he took it back to the sofa with him. "You're too uptight, dude," he said, taking an enormous hit off it. He held the smoke in for a long moment before continuing. "You need to relax, kick back. Grace is still here, you know. Grace will set you straight."

I wanted to argue about being uptight, but thoughts of Grace flooded my mind. She'd slept with everyone in the house while I lived there, and sometimes there were a lot of us. We called her as Amazing Grace – and for obvious reasons. It wasn't that she was loose or anything like that, those being the days of free-love or not. No, Grace thought of herself as a healer, a sexual healer. Man, did she heal. If you were down, she'd make you happy. If you were happy, she'd make you ecstatic. She was just amazing, through and through.

As if on cue, Grace came in from the kitchen carrying a tea tray with a large, earthenware teapot on it. The tea's aroma was unmistakable: Lapsang Souchong, her old favorite: so heady and so smoky that I caught a whiff of it even over the smell of dope in the air.

Grace, herself, was just as heady and smoky as ever. Still so sultry and hot that I couldn't believe the number of years since I'd last seen her.

"Matt!" She set the tea tray on the coffee table, and came straight over to me, her long raven-colored hair flecked with a bit of gray, but her skin as smooth as ever, hardly a wrinkle, her dark eyes radiant, and her curves moving as only her curves could.

"Grace—" I tried to stand, but her hands were already on my shoulders, gently pushing me back down, her masseuse-like fingers lightly working into my tight muscles.

"It's been a long time, Matt," she said, bending over and kissing me flush on the lips. As she did so, the loose top of her yellow sundress revealed that she was braless as ever, and still had tantalizingly perfect breasts, tanned as the rest of her since she always sunbathed in the nude.

She knew I'd been looking, smiled and tousled my hair, then sat on the edge of my armchair and put one arm around my shoulder. She didn't say anything else, had never been one for many words, preferred to let her body do the talking, was into something she called Tantric love, which she once explained as prolonging any lovemaking session far beyond what anybody would call great sex, building and building like a fugue toward new heights of intimacy and the divine.

"Matt was just telling me that somebody's killing our old buddies from Nam,"Boo told her, not a trace of worry in his voice as he sucked down more dope.

"That's not good," said Grace. She said it like a throw-away line, like it was of no consequence because it was negative. I knew where she was going – Grace believed we controlled our own karma – and she sure did. If something was bad, she'd make it good, and if something was good, she'd make it even better. "So that's why you're uptight," Grace told me. She got up, took the joint from Boo, then sat back down with me and took a hit before passing it to me. "This will balance you, Matt. I can feel your karma, just like I felt the tension across your shoulders."

I stared at the joint in front of me. The weed's familiar smell as alluring as Grace. What the hell… I was in the time-machine, again, with Grace and Boo – those long-ago days of fuck it, no worries, drawing me back – everything about the old house in Fairhaven so much the same, and telling me why not, screw it, you need a break.

So, I took the joint and inhaled deeply; held my breath before blowing it back out, the 'good shit' working fast, making me want more and more as I took additional hits and could feel it was way stronger than what we had back in the day, and knew I shouldn't, but didn't care.

Grace took the joint from me, toked up again, then handed it back to Boo.

"B.C. Bud," said Boo. "The best."

"Yeah," I said as it worked its old black magic on me.

"Yeah," echoed Grace. "Come with me, Matt." She took my hand and led me toward the back door, which was off the kitchen. As we left, Boo, utterly stoned and stretched out across the sofa like a well-fed cat, said, "See, Matt? No worries. No worries at all."

I'd smoked enough to almost agree with him, but the instant we stepped outside, I took in my surroundings at a glance, alert for any sound or movement.

"You're still tense, Matt," said Grace, squeezing my hand. "Come on, I'll fix that." She pulled me forward, her eyes gleaming. "Let's go to the dome."

It was hard to resist Grace. I let her take me down the short, brick path leading to the geodesic dome that Boo had built in 1970. I hadn't thought about the dome in years. Everybody had wanted to stay in it, and everybody did at one time or another.

It was still too cool, I thought, standing in front of it with Grace. Boo had built it out of a kit, probably from the Whole Earth Catalog. It was about 12 feet tall and 12 feet in diameter, hexagonal in shape, with a skylight at its top, where the moon and stars seemed to dance on a love filled night. Something about being in its curved interior always gave me an otherworldly feeling. Especially when I was stoned. Even more when I was stoned and having sex.

Part of me couldn't believe that I'd fallen to the old Mary Jane again. I thought I left it far behind. But this new B.C. Bud was potent as hell, sensuously mellow and damned fine. Like Grace, who stood beside me, hardly changed over all the years, still so alluring, promising bliss and abandon and just fuck all the troubles, get laid, take the edge off, screw your brains out forever, feel good, feel better, get even higher and float above it all and to hell with everything…

…floating on the waterbed in the middle of the dome – smooth goose down comforter – Grace's silken, hot skin – the blue sky and clouds sailing above – then candles flickering, and sandalwood incense burning – more tokes on more jays – now stars twinkling – night songs and crickets – where the day went, no matter – and more sex to the strains of Hendrix's Purple Haze as we meld to a delicious mix of she and me and no telling where either of us begin or end…

"Man, I feel good."

"I knew you would."

She goes down on me again.

Amazing Grace… No worries… No Nam… Just now…

Chapter Fourteen

I woke slowly, feeling free and easy, utterly relaxed. Didn't remember where I was, but didn't care – I felt at peace, the smell of last night's pot hanging heavy in the air, the morning sun streaming through the skylight, warm and comforting, almost caressing me where it fell on my bare chest. Grace lay on her stomach beside me, sleeping in the nude. The soft, goose down comforter was pushed down to her feet, revealing her smooth, lithe back and her perfectly rounded bottom.

Man, it just doesn't get better than this, I thought.

As if she heard my mental compliment, Grace's left arm slid over my chest, and her hand gently squeezed my side. I sighed, felt like I could stay there forever.

Then I sat straight up in bed. Knew exactly where I was and what I'd done. All the old feelings rushed back, replacing the warm-fuzzy's with a jittery, nervous tension. It was in a trap! The worst kind of trap. The phony sex and drug-filled trap that I'd barely escaped years ago before it destroyed me.

Grace, startled by my sudden movement, woke up and sleepily said, "Matt… What's going on? What are you doing?"

I didn't answer. Had to get out of there. Jumped out of bed and threw my clothes on, afraid to hardly look at her, afraid that what I saw would suck me right back in.

"Matt," she said again, getting up and coming toward me.

I'm out of here!" I told her.

I ran around the house and piled into my car – hit the freeway back to Seattle – pushed the Firebird to ninety – needed the speed; it matched the way I felt. I was breathing fast and shallow, my heart racing, my thoughts bouncing all over and not making much sense. It was the damned dope. Marijuana began having that effect on me years ago when I was still using. I'd feel great for a while, then get nervous, agitated, felt like I was coming apart. I don't know why, just that it seemed like everything was suddenly trying to catch up with me.

I could handle it, I told myself, my hands sweaty on the steering wheel. My head was spinning – I could control it – sure I could.

I hit the brakes. Hit them hard, went into a drift across two lanes, almost spun out, then finally came to a stop on the shoulder of the road. I had to get out. Had to get away. Jumped out of the car and ran – ran like my life depended on it.

It was Nam all over again – the panic – the running away...

Guard duty again. I'm in the foxhole with Shabazz. Shouldn't talk on guard duty, so we whisper. He's going on and on about the 'Man,' and how he's stuck over here fighting the white man's war, and then rambles on about the Black Panthers and Huey Newton and Black Power and Elijah Mohammed and the Black Muslims and how the Panthers ought to get together with the Black Muslims and really stick it to the 'Man.'

One of our Claymores goes off! Then another. They've hit the tripwires outside our perimeter. "They're in the wire! They're in the wire!" I scream. Pitch black, can't see a thing, except their muzzle-flashes as they charge us, bullets pinging around our foxhole.

"Motherfuckers!" yells Shabazz -- my mind's racing – he's firing – I'm firing – more flashes as the Cong hit more of our booby-traps...

Everybody's shooting up and down the line, fifty yards to the left and right. I empty my second clip at them – they're still coming – I knock a few dark shapes down, but they're still coming! Screams and cries!

"Up!" yells Shabazz. He grabs me, pulls me up while still firing. "We gotta fall back, get better cover!" I'm up on my feet, out of the foxhole – they're all around us – we're running – running – running!

I trip – he helps me up – a grenade lands close by – Shabazz screams, "Grenade!" – shoves me away from it and tackles me to the ground,

...then a booming rush of air – and silence – total silence – except for the ringing in my ears...

...and Shabazz's cries of pain – he's beside me – he's grabbing the back of his left leg – "fuck and fuck!" he yells...

...then the Cong are gone – just like that, they hit and run – everybody's sounding off – a medic shoots Shabazz up with morphine – checks my ears, says I'm OK...

...but Shabazz isn't – they've called for a Medi-vac – his calf muscle's torn up from the shrapnel – chopper will be in to pick him up...

"I'm sorry, man," I say, kneeling beside him – "You saved my life – I'm sorry..."

"Ha!" he says, looking up at me, high on the morphine. "Don't be sorry – I got a million-dollar wound, baby – I'm outa this fucked up war – medic says it's bad but not too bad – should heal up in a couple months – I'm a short-timer, won't heal fast enough for them to send me back – I'm going home!"

I crank up the Firebird and merge into traffic. I still feel like running. I know just where I'm going to run down to Oakland and see Shabazz, who's just plain Luther Brown again. *Councilman Brown* at that. Owe him. Gotta warn him. Make sure he's safe.

• • •

I kept thinking about Grace on the plane to Oakland. Couldn't help it. So, I was glad to get my little bottle of whiskey from the flight attendant – Grace was like drugs, so good you naturally wanted more -- if you tried to quit, the only way to get her out of your system was to replace her with something else. I sipped at the whiskey and turned my attention to the clouds outside my window seat. Billowy, white, swirling, a patch of bright blue here and there. They were very much like the clouds were on my flight into Nam back in the day. When we had finally descended through them, the vivid, green canopy of the jungle came into view and I remember thinking, *man, that's beautiful, really gorgeous, like a tropical paradise – never saw anything like this before.* Then we landed in Saigon and I was thrown straight into the shit of war: *yeah, man, you know it: you sure as hell never saw anything like that before.*

I got a second drink and tried to think about something good. Rachel was O.K., Jessica was better than O.K., the insurance on my houseboat would eventually kick in, and I'd bought my first cell phone, so I could stay in touch, even though I hadn't figured out quite how to use it. I'd also bought change of clothes before leaving, still had a few Hendrix tapes left in my car, and about all my remaining worldly possessions in the small suitcase I'd bought for my trip. What more could anybody want?

• • •

San Francisco International was busy, people hustling to and fro, a few folks here and there with glazed eyes and sagging expressions, like they'd been delayed or missed a flight, but most in a hurry, like me.

I found a halfway quiet spot in one of the waiting areas, and took out my cell phone. I needed to call Rachel and let her know how to reach me. Stupid tiny numbers on the phone were a pain to use, but I finally got her number punched in right.

"Hey, Rachel," I said when she answered. "Time for you to get a gun."

"What?"

"I just bought a cell phone," I said with a chuckle. "I'm in the airport in San Francisco. On my way over to Oakland. Going to hang out with Councilman Brown. Let him know what's going on."

"Did you talk to Tanaka?" she asked.

"What are you, my Mom?" I laughed – kind of nervously, actually – didn't really know why I said that, as I hardly talked about my Mom since she passed a few years back. "Anyway," I went on. "Figured I needed a way to stay in touch. So, if I'm going to embrace technology, then you should get a gun."

"A cell phone is hardly technology, Matt, it's— "

"Damn, I hate this thing," I said, fumbling a bit with the too-small phone. "Can't really talk on it very well. Look, here's my number." I read the number to her. "Like I told you, I'm on my way to Oakland. Call me if you need me."

"OK, be safe," she said.

I closed the phone; almost dropped it. I just wasn't used to talking on something so small. So, I found a bank of pay phones, and dialed Oakland City Hall, trying to reach Shabazz again. Like the previous calls before I left Seattle, all I got was his receptionist telling me that Councilman Brown was unavailable, and did I care to leave a message?

"I've already left a couple messages for him," I told her. "Do you know if he got them? This is Matt Rossiter."

"Oh yes, Mr. Rossiter, I remember talking to you. I don't know if he got your messages or not. It's been very hectic with the councilman preparing for his news conference today."

"What news conference? When?"

"In about an hour and a half," she said.

"Where?"

"He's holding it downtown, at Preservation Park," she told me.

I caught a cab from the airport and headed to Oakland. Had plenty of time to get to Shabazz's news conference, especially since the cab driver drove like a bat out of hell – which I didn't mind – the guy was a good driver and I liked the speed. We reached the Bay Bridge in hardly any time at all.

I hadn't been to Oakland since I'd shipped out to Nam from the Oakland Army Terminal almost thirty years ago. You'd think with all the time elapsed, that it would be no big deal. But as soon as we hit the city, I started getting whispers and anxious pangs like I had while waiting to leave for the war. I tried to ride them out, but they got louder and stranger with every mile we drove.

I kept thinking about the last time I was in San Francisco's poor relation across the bay, and the trip I took to the war with countless others. Above all, I remembered feeling lonely. The worst kind of lonely. The kind that seeps into your pores and permeates every cell in your body, until you reached a point where you could be standing in a huge crowd, but still felt like you were the last person on earth.

Two days before I shipped out, I got my final pass from the transit company I was in, and went into town and ended up just wandering the streets looking for anything that could take my mind off where I'd soon be going. I must have walked ten miles or so, but didn't find a thing that helped.

I was in uniform, didn't think I needed to bring any civvies, because I thought I'd be heading right off to Vietnam. Had no idea that it took days to get processed, and get all the shots and vaccinations, etc.

About mid-day, the fog had burned off, and I was getting kind of hot – it sure was warmer in the bay area than Seattle at that time of the year. I passed the Greyhound Bus depot and thought I'd take a break. Got a Coke and took it back outside and sat on one of the benches on the street where some folks were waiting to catch one of the city transit buses. I found a spot between an elderly black couple and a long-haired hippie who wore a tie-dyed shirt, blue beads around his neck, and open-toed sandals on his bare feet. He had a big transistor radio, the volume of which was turned way up. Just as I sat down, a new song began to play Simon and Garfunkel's 'The Sounds of Silence.'

It was weird. Here I was, surrounded people and city traffic and various other noise, but was still feeling so alone. That song described how I felt much better than I could ever put in words.

Halfway through the tune, a city bus pulled up. A few people got off, then it began to board new passengers. The black couple got on first, then the hippie followed, but paused in the bus's open doorway. He turned around, looked directly at me, then threw me the V-shaped peace sign. "Peace and love, brother," he told me. "Peace and love."

A day and a half later, I went to war.

Chapter Fifteen

The grey-haired, pony-tailed cab driver had been blabbing non-stop ever since I mentioned how many years had gone by since I'd last been to Oakland. He'd launched into sight-seeing mode telling me how much the city had changed and pointed out all the new buildings and developments along the way. His high-pitched voice and rapid-fire delivery reminded me of a mosquito buzzing around my ear. Didn't help my mood any, and I got edgier by the minute.

This is stupid, I told myself. It's just a town like any other. You'll go see Magic, warn him, then head back to the airport. Simple. No sweat.

But visions of the Army Terminal kept dancing before my eyes: the endless processing; all the shots and vaccinations; and my temporary bunk with all the other temporary soldiers, all of us hoping our lives wouldn't be temporary once we got to Vietnam. Until we got our orders for transit, we acted in three different ways; nervous, full of bravado, or totally silent on the subject. For myself, I think I acted all three ways.

"Yeah," the cab driver went on. "This town has finally started to change. We've even got zillionaires' houses up in the hills now, can you believe it? Got some new office buildings nice as any in San Francisco. Lots of folks think this town is going places, it's— "

"The Oakland Army Terminal is near here, isn't it?" I interrupted, deciding it was best to face the demon that was biting me.

"Huh?" he asked like it was rude to break into his monologue. "Yeah," he said, glancing over his shoulder at me. "It's close enough."

"Take me there," I told him.

"Well, it *is* a little out of the way."

"I don't care."

He shut up for a while as he computed the best route to the new destination. Wasn't long, though, before he was back at it pointing out all the places of interest anew.

The old army base was close to the Oakland side of the bridge, and we got there fairly quickly. It was virtually abandoned now, and I remembered reading that it would be permanently closed down shortly. Not much left of it even now, except the athletic field, acres of empty barracks, and the old Admin Building in front of the post.

When we arrived there, the white, monolithic Admin Building struck me the same way it had when I first saw it: like some giant waiting to suck me in and chew me up. The old howitzer standing in front of it pointed directly at my taxi, like it was advertising that I was still under the gun and death could come at any moment.

I felt a little shaky. Got out of the cab, leaned up against it, and had a smoke as I gazed up at the edifice that loomed larger and larger the more I stared at it.

The cab driver got out and joined me. He was quiet for a bit as he rolled a cigarette from some Drum tobacco.

Lighting it, he asked, "Were you in Nam?"

"Yeah."

"Thought so," he said, taking the cigarette out of his mouth with nicotine-stained fingers, then spitting out a bit of loose tobacco. "You're not the first one who's had me drive here. Been lots of them over the years."

"That right?"

"Hell yes. Tons of 'em. Me, this is my hometown. I can't help but see it from time to time. Finally got used to it, though. Even got a civilian job at the Terminal for a while when I first got back."

"You were in Nam, too?" I asked.

"Uh-huh." He looked away from me, out over the expanse of the nearly deserted Army Terminal. "Tet," he said. "A bitch."

"I got there after the Tet Offensive," I told him.

"You're lucky," he said. "That was some real bullshit."

I didn't say anything. There was nothing to say.

"Weed was good, though," he said. "I'll give Nam that."

I nodded the affirmative.

"You know, they're going to close this for good."

"That's what I heard."

"Yeah. Next month, end of September, it'll be history. I'm proud of my service, but good riddance to it, anyway."

We finished our smokes in silence, me thinking – and maybe him, too – about the soldiers who began their journeys here, but never made it back.

It was time to hit the road. I'd seen all I'd needed to see. It was past. Done. Fuck it.

Just as I turned to get back in the cab, the driver smiled at me, and said, "You seem to be doing OK with this. I've had some guys here break down and cry." Then he offered me his hand along with the standard Nam-vet to Nam-vet line, "Glad you made it back, bud."

"Same-same," I told him, and shook his hand.

There was a crowd gathered when I stepped out of the cab at Preservation Park, a small neighborhood of beautifully restored Victorian homes, set around a lovely square with a large, tall fountain in the middle of it. The palm trees and other complimenting foliage made the area seem like a lush oasis set right in the heart of downtown Oakland.

Over a hundred people were gathered in the square, the majority of them black, which matched the Oakland I remembered from my brief time there. It had always been a blue collar, mostly African American city across the bay from San Francisco.

What didn't jibe with my memory, though, were all the improvements to the town since back in the day. The downtown area had gone from looking rundown, to many parts of it seeming almost upscale, with new buildings, restored older buildings, nice restaurants and shopping areas, and the fine looking, Preservation Park where the cab driver took me. Even the nearby high-rises were very new. They were a few blocks away, overlooking the square, and looked to have been built recently.

Shabazz had a hand in putting Preservation Park put together in the 1980's, according to the cabby. He had been instrumental in many of the other improvements to Oakland as well over the years, including helping to arrange political support and financing for a great many projects. Like he was doing today – announcing the go-ahead for one of his pet projects, the conversion of the once decrepit Thomas Block into over three-hundred units of low-income housing.

"Wish I could hang around for the news conference," the cabby told me as he dropped me off. "Councilman Brown has done a hell of a job for this city, but I got another fare waiting for me."

I worked my way up to the front of the crowd, past the couple news crews covering the event, and near the raised platform by the fountain that faced high-rise buildings. The platform had obviously been put up just for the councilman's appearance. Only three people were 'on stage' at the moment: a guy setting up the microphone at the podium in the middle of the platform, and two Black Panthers standing on either side, stationed at each set of short stairs the led up to the platform itself. They wore the classic garb – black leather jackets over dark pants, with black berets on their heads – even had afros under their berets like back in the day.

I hadn't seen or heard much about the Black Panthers for ages. They'd scared the hell out of white America in the 60's, and were faulted for a lot of violence, most of which they hadn't committed. They had begun in Oakland and that's where they essentially ended when the Oakland police set them up and massacred many of them. Of course, that fact only came out years later, but by then the Panthers were a spent force for all intents and purposes. With all the hype and bad press about them, however, most folks had little knowledge of the good they did, and kept on doing, right up to the present day: helping with educational opportunities and free food programs for kids and such.

For myself, I'd had hardly any contact with black people in Seattle. I remember telling my dad, who I saw only every now and then, that all the riots that were going on were really wrong and how could people do that shit.

He surprised me, said, "Yeah, that's bullshit all right, but what would you do if you didn't have much of anything and you thought people were trying to take it away? I'd start throwing bricks myself, son. Either that or maybe pick up a gun."

Anyway, my progress toward the front of the crowd had picked up the attention of the two Black Panthers on the stage. Both eyed me intently, evidently wondering if I was a threat. I gave them a small smile. They didn't return it.

Then Shabazz appeared from the other side of the fountain, applauded by the throng as he approached the platform to speak. Even though I hadn't seen him in years, I recognized him immediately. He was still tall and lean, hadn't filled out at all between Nam and now. His hair was cut short, though, no more big afro like he had back then, but he had grown a closely-trimmed, short goatee. And he was wearing a suit and tie – blue, pinstriped, tailored suit with a sparkling white shirt and maroon colored tie. He looked every inch the successful banker and city councilman. The only thing that seemed out of place, was his being a Republican city councilman in a heavily Democrat city.

He was about twenty feet away from me when he climbed up onto the platform.

"Shabazz!" I yelled. "Hey, Shabazz!"

Startled, he looked my way, and I added, "It's me, Matt Rossiter!"

He paused, looked directly into my eyes, then smiled. "Matt," he said, "Matt Rossiter. Too much. What are you doing here?"

"We gotta talk," I told him, as the two Black Panthers nervously converged and flanked Shabazz. They both stared bullets at me. "You're in danger, man," I told my old comrade.

"Yeah?" he asked, then glanced around, as did his security when they overheard me. "Well, I've got a speech to give," he said. "Hell, come on up here and join me. We can talk after."

I went to the stairs on the left side of the platform. As I did, I heard somebody behind me say, "Who the hell's that guy?"

The Panther nearest me moved aside as I gained the platform. Shabazz came over and met me, shook my hand and patted my shoulder. "You're a little huskier, Matt," he said in a hushed tone, keeping our conversation private. "Looking good, though. You living here now?"

"No, still in Seattle." I kept my voice low, too. "I'm a private investigator."

"You? I'll be damned."

"Look," I told him. "I'm here to warn you. There's somebody killing off our old squad."

"No shit?"

"No shit."

A look of concern crossed his face, then he gave me a wry smile. "OK," he said. "We'll talk about it. First, I've got to give my speech. Just hang loose on the side there, I won't be that long."

He didn't give me a chance to argue, just went straight to the mike, the Black Panthers positioning themselves about ten feet from him on either side.

"Friends and constituents," Shabazz began. "I welcome you here on this fine day. I've got exciting news on the Thomas Block. But first, I want to talk about our fair city of Oakland. We've always gotten a bad rap compared to our big, rich brother on the other side of the bay. Got one of the highest crime rates in the nation. Why is that?"

"Criminals!" yelled somebody in the crowd. There was a murmur of laughter as another person added, "Too many criminals!"

"Right on!" boomed Shabazz, as if he expected the answer. "What makes a criminal? Are they just born that way? Does God say, 'Well son, *you're* going to be good and *you're* going to be bad, and I'm going to put most of you bad ones in Oakland and most of you good ones in San Francisco.' Is that it?"

"No!" came a shout from the crowd.

Shabazz smiled, then paused. "Is it because they're *black*?" he asked pointedly.

A number of folks voiced their loud disapproval.

"A majority of Oakland's population is black," he continued, his voice building in intensity. "But there are less than ten percent of Afro-Americans on our police force. Why is that? Why is that?"

"Racism!" came his answer.

"There is that," said Shabazz. "There is always that. But there's something else and I'll tell you what it is. It's because so many black applicants to our police department have criminal records and can't qualify. That leads me back to the original question: what makes a criminal?" he fairly screamed. "It's lack of education, lack of opportunity, poverty, not having enough to eat or a decent place to live!" he roared.

Shabazz was still a firebrand, I thought, same guy I knew in Nam but much better dressed.

"So," he continued, "I'll return to the good news about the Thomas Block. We're soon going to add more low-income housing here in Oakland. It's been formally approved by the full city council! Over 300 apartments for low income and the disadvantaged."

This drew a huge applause, then more and more applause as he continued, extolling the virtues of redevelopment, government grants, expanded food programs, and low-interest loans, and his part in putting it all together, just as he'd done when he spearheaded the creation of Preservation Park. He also added a bit about the next mayoral and city council elections.

Me, I was nervous looking out over the crowd. Every time a flash went off from a photographer, I couldn't help think it might be something else. This was the perfect setup for anybody looking to off Shabazz. He was out in the open; his security wouldn't do much good if somebody tried to waste him. So I edged a little closer to him as he spoke.

Something glinted in the sunlight across the square! Looked like It came from the roof of the nearest high-rise. The instant it glinted again, I knew exactly what it had to be the scope on a rifle!

"Gun!" I yelled. I sprinted to shield Shabazz, but a Black Panther got in front of him first, and took a bullet in the back for his effort, a mist of bright blood puffing out of his leather jacket. Screams from the crowd as another rifle-shot sounded just as I tackled Shabazz and pulled him down. A searing pain ripped through my right side, but at least I'd gotten him out of the line of fire.

Or, I thought I had. Pandemonium ensuing, everybody ducking and running, the other Panther formed a human shield in front of Shabazz and me. I stayed put on top of him, trying to protect him. Then I heard him groan, saw blood on my hands, a bloody crease across my ribs, and frothy blood gurgling out of Shabazz's mouth.

Damn! He'd been shot. Bullet must have sliced along my side and hit him as I tackled him.

"Shabazz," I said, looking into his eyes that were going all glassy.

"Hell, Matt," he managed, his face contorted with pain. "You brought…the war…with you…"

Chapter Sixteen

I got a few stitches at the hospital – I was lucky, the bullet had only creased the side of my ribs. Shabazz wasn't so lucky. He was fighting for his life in surgery while the police questioned me about my involvement. I gave them a recap about the sonofabitch who was trying to kill off my old squad. No, I didn't know who he was, but I'd sure let them know if I found out and he was still alive after I got to him. In the meantime, if they needed anything else, they could contact Lieutenant Dale Tanaka at the Seattle Police Department.

My cellphone had rung while I was getting fixed up. I knew it had voicemail, so I didn't answer it. When I finally got around to it, though, I couldn't figure out how to access my voicemail. I asked one of the nurses if she knew how. She smiled, then got my voicemail up easy as you please.

It was a message from Rachel. She'd found an address for Smitty, in Astoria, Oregon. Told me to be safe and she'd be in touch.

Another detective came up to me just then. Told me to stick around town – they'd probably have more questions for me.

So, I told him I would, then left the hospital and took a cab straight to the airport. I booked a flight to Portland, Oregon – near as I could get to Astoria on the Oregon coast, where, according to the info Rachel had given me, my old buddy, Smitty, was currently living. He was the only other guy besides Boo who had treated me decently when I was still the numero uno cherry in our platoon. I needed to warn him quick as I could because his was the next name on the list after Shabazz. Calling him had done no good – I just kept getting a busy signal every time I'd tried – right up to finishing my last shot of Wild Turkey in the airport lounge. My flight wasn't until the morning, and I was beat. So, I caught some much-needed Z's in the waiting area and barely woke up in time to catch my plane.

I tried calling Smitty again when we touched down in Portland. And once more, before renting a car at the airport. Smitty's phone being busy for so long worried me. Maybe it had just been political assassination attempt against Shabazz, but I didn't think so. It was too damned coincidental with everything that had been going down. As I drove west out of Portland, I hoped nobody had gotten to Smitty before I could.

I'd rented a 5.0 litre Mustang. Fastest car I could get. It wasn't as quick as my Firebird, but I punched it up pretty good as I sped along the Columbia River toward its mouth in Astoria. The further I got out of Portland, the more unpopulated it became. Pretty soon, except for the occasional logging truck that I passed, it was just me and the forest and the constantly winding and dipping road, the centerline becoming a blur when I gunned it on the straightaways.

It was one of those drives that couldn't over quick enough. I found my thoughts wandering a bit during eighty-odd miles that never seemed to end. Although I'd never been religious, I said a few prayers for Shabazz and Smitty. It was funny, but like in Nam, prayer came easily if you were feeling desperate. And Nam itself came back all too easily during the drive.

I'm in a very large village again. An Loc or Phuc Vinh, I don't remember which. It doesn't matter. What matters is that we've got a three-hour pass. Smitty and me and Camacho, the sergeant from another squad in our platoon, 1st squad. We've got a pass. Three hours away from the war. At least, away from the platoon, considering we're still in the middle of fucking Nam. We've got three hours to pretend there isn't a war – to be like tourists, see the sights – three hours to do whatever we want.

"What do you want to do?" I ask Smitty and sergeant Camacho.

"Get laid," says Camacho.

"Get some real food," says Smitty. "Fuck all these C-Rations -- a big, juicy steak."

"A big, juicy Conchita," counters Camacho, "that's what I want."

"What about you, Rossiter?" Smitty asks. "What do you want?"

"Both," I say, trying to sound like I know what I'm doing. Hell, I don't even know where I am, let alone what to do. We've walked maybe half a mile or so, into this big village, which is more like a real town. I'm all turned around, completely lost, but I don't care. This is a big place. Over fifteen thousand people, somebody told me. There's an old town square up ahead that's fronted by a two-story, French Colonial style building – I can't read the Vietnamese sign on it, but I imagine it's the city hall or something like that.

Man, if I forget about all the cheap, tin hooches and little bamboo kiosks that are all over the place, I can almost believe I'm in a small town back home. It has streets, mostly unpaved, real buildings, mostly one or two-story, ramshackle affairs, and there's traffic, lots of motor scooters everywhere, and people, civilians, walking around just like they're taking in a nice summer day, except you think you're going to die if you let yourself think about the heat and humidity too much.

"Com'on," says Smitty, "let's find a restaurant."

"And a whorehouse," says Camacho. "Steak and pussy. Mmnn–mmnn! Sounds good, huh, Rossiter?"

"Yeah."

I say "yeah" but I don't know if I really mean it. A steak sounds great if we can find it, but the whorehouse thing... I've never done anything like that. It sounds exciting in a way, but kind of uncomfortable, too. I should do it, though. It's what you're supposed to do over here, I guess.

"We gotta get some jays, first," says Camacho.

"Where are we going to get that?" I ask.

"Man, don't you know anything?" says Camacho. "You're such a cherry-ass."

"Mary Jane's everywhere over here," Smitty tells me. "You'll learn." He's trying to be helpful, and I appreciate it. Smitty's been in-country for more than four months – he's about the only one who's treated me decently since I got here.

"He better learn," Camacho frowns. "You'll fuck up and get somebody's ass toasted someday if you don't, Rossiter." He shakes his head. Then he smiles and says, "Fuck it. Today we get high. Follow me."

Camacho leads the way to the nearest kiosk on the street. It's like all the others, a couple of the skinny, bamboo stands on every corner, all of them selling cigarettes and warm pop and beer.

"Gimmee a pack of Camels," Camacho tells the old Vietnamese woman in the kiosk. She reaches around to her display of smokes and starts to get the pack of Camels. "No," says Camacho. "The 'special' Camels."

The old woman nods her head, reaches under the small counter and takes out a pack of Camels, which she hands over.

We walk off after Camacho pays her, opening the cigarette pack as we go.

"I thought we were buying some dope," I say.

Camacho turns to me with a big shit-eating grin. He hands us both of us one of the smokes.

"What's this?" I ask. "It's just a cigarette."

"Smell it," Camacho tells me.

I do as he says. I'm surprised as can be when the perfectly rolled Camel-straight turns out to be filled with weed instead of tobacco. "Damn, it's filled with dope," I say.

"Shit's great," Smitty says.

"No shit," Camacho tells him, lighting up his phony Camel and sucking in a deep drag and holding the sweet-smelling smoke as long as he can before blowing it out. "Good shit," he says. Then he turns to me and explains, "The gooks take regular cigarettes, empty the tobacco out and fill them back up with weed. Then they put the cellophane on the pack again and who's to know they're not regular Camels or Lucky's or Pall Mall's, huh? You can smoke 'em anywhere, even around officers."

"Smart," says Smitty. "These gooks are smart."

I take a hit, but cup my smoke in my hand, feeling a little nervous doing it out in public.

"Fuck, Rossiter," says Camacho, slapping my hand. "Enjoy it, man! Nobody knows. Nobody cares, either – it's Nam, cherry."

Two hits and I feel it right off the bat – suck down some more and close my eyes and I'm far away.

"Let's di di," says Camacho, grabbing my arm. "We've only got two and a half hours left. Gotta make the most of it."

"I've got the munchies already," says Smitty.

I laugh my ass off at that. It's good to laugh, and it's like a dream as we move down the street. First time I've felt good since I've been in Nam. I don't even feel tired anymore. I always feel tired. Never get any sleep. Don't give a shit now.

Smitty stops, points across the road at a low, tan, stucco building just a little bigger than a two-car garage. A few people are visible sitting at tables through its front window. "Look, a restaurant. That's a restaurant, isn't it?"

"And a whorehouse," says Camacho.

"Where's a whorehouse?" I ask. "All I see is that restaurant."

"What do you think that is, cherry?" says Camacho, pointing just to the right of the restaurant at the small building adjoining it. There's a line of soldiers, maybe a dozen or so, snaking out from the end of it.

"A line for the restaurant?" I ask.

"My ass," Camacho tells me. "Troops don't line up like that for a hunk of fucking water buffalo they call steak. That's a line for some real meat, baby."

"I'm still hungry," says Smitty, the last of his jay just a small roach that gives up one last toke before he tosses it down.

"Screw first, eat later," Camacho tells him, then heads for the line outside what he says is the whorehouse. "Com'on, fall in with me boys," he tells us. "Sloppy seconds is better than nothin' at all."

We follow Camacho and get in line. It moves faster than I would have thought, half the soldiers ahead of us talking shit, and some quiet like me, just looking straight ahead as we move up in order. Camacho's already lit another jay and been telling us about this chick in Yuma that he's going to marry when he gets out of Nam. Smitty joins in about his girlfriend who's waiting for him. Me, I don't have a girlfriend, so I make one up – call her 'Jan' – tell them that she's got dark hair and blue eyes and is really good in bed, even though I've never been to bed with a woman before.

The line moves forward, one at a time – one soldier in, one soldier out, most of them smiling as they do so. Pretty soon, it's Camacho's turn. He's been all animated, talking shit and happy as hell, but gets serious and quiet as he goes through the colored beads that hang down from the doorway to the whorehouse.

I'm next – I'm high and nervous. I make myself smile when Smitty slaps me on the back and tells me to live it up. I can do this. I have to do this. If I don't, I'll never fit in.

Then out comes Camacho, grinning like the Cheshire Cat, whooping it up and telling us it's the best he ever had.

I hesitate.

One of the soldiers who have gotten into line behind us yells, "Move it buddy! Move it or lose it!"

In I go. It's halfway dark inside. Still hot, but a little cooler than outside. This young girl, maybe twelve, sticks out her hand and says, "Two dollar." And I give her the money and she points across the room – a much smaller place than I thought it would be – and there's a dirty mattress in the middle of it – and a naked woman, in her thirties I think, laying on her back on the mattress – and she's staring blankly at the ceiling – and the place smells like fish and incense – and the girl who took my money goes off to the left and goes behind a wall that's made of beer cans that have been put together somehow, end to end, like a metal screen you can see through…

…but I can't see the girl behind the beer can wall anymore – and I approach the naked woman and say hello – and she says nothing, just keeps staring up at the ceiling – and I do what I have to and pull my pants down and get on top of her…

…and I'm doing it and not feeling good – she's like a corpse under me – doesn't move at all – and I keep at it, but don't know if I can finish…

…and then I hear laughter – I glance over at the beer can wall – a very old woman, and the twelve-year-old girl, are visible through it – and they are laughing and tittering and giggling as they look straight at me like I'm their TV...

…and I'm up on my feet and pull on my pants – and I'm out of there – and I force a smile when I see Smitty – but I feel much worse than before I went in…

…and I'm happy to get back to the war.

The next day, Smitty got both of his legs blown off.

Chapter Seventeen

I pulled off the road at the first wide spot I found – pulled off pretty fast, too, considering the cloud of dust the Mustang sent up when it came to a stop. I was covered with sweat despite the car's air conditioning.

Fuck it… Just fuck it!

I got out and tried to take a deep breath – felt like I was hyperventilating. I finally got my breath back, and saw that I'd stopped in the first sign of civilization I'd seen for miles. It wasn't much, just a restaurant on my side of the highway that had a big sign advertising, "Famous pies, jams & jellies." Down below the restaurant, on the bank of the wide Columbia River, were a few well-worn wooden buildings that made up whatever tiny town this was.

The outside thermometer by the restaurant door read 90 degrees. There was a Coke machine outside the place. I got a can and pressed it against my forehead. It felt so good that I thought it would be a shame to drink it.

I took my phone out, fucked with it a bit before I got it working, then tried to call Smitty. Getting only a damned busy signal again, I hit the road.

I covered the last twenty miles or so into Astoria in record time. I'd read somewhere that it was the oldest town on the entire west coast, and it sure looked it. It had been founded by some trading company right after the Lewis & Clark expedition, and had definitely seen better days. Going due west, the main drag – only about three-quarters of a mile long – had a few old, low, brick buildings, a large furniture store that needed a fresh coat of paint, and a used car lot that was heavy with older model pick-up trucks. Here and there, on the south side of the street, were a few large and dilapidated Victorian houses, only one of which had been restored anything like its former glory. To the north, the Columbia spread out miles wide at its mouth and was bisected by an enormous, high bridge that spanned the great river's tremendous width across to the Washington state side.

The main drag turned sharply to the south just under the steep concrete onramp leading up to the bridge proper. I spotted Smitty's street about a block before I got to the bridge. I turned and rolled down the steep and potholed pavement about three blocks, until the road dead ended at a weathered bulkhead just above the river. Smitty's house was perched a few feet to the right of the dead end, where it overlooked the Columbia. If there was a wrong side of town in Astoria, this was it, I thought, when I got out of the car.

Gulls keened overhead, and the sound of a ship's horn blared from one of the many freighters plying the mighty river, as I surveyed Smitty's place. It was a squat and square little house with weathered clapboard siding. The roof was some ancient green composition material, patched here and there with darker green or rust colored roofing. The red brick chimney leaned off center, as did the house itself on its badly settled foundation. The windows were small and narrow, framed in peeling wood, and it had an old oil barrel attached to the side of it, rather than a more modern underground tank for its furnace's fuel. At best, it had been some worker's cottage around the turn of the century, like the couple other dilapidated houses above it on the steep hillside. At worst, well, what you saw was what you got, even though the view alone would have been worth a million bucks in Seattle.

A gently sloping paved path led up to the house through what front yard there was. Somebody had worked on the yard – it was bordered by bright, yellow flowers, and the house had pretty red geraniums in window boxes. After being unable to help Shabazz, and Smitty's name being next on the list, I approached the front door warily, listening for any sound of trouble. I slowly went up the short ramp that served for steps to the porch. I kept telling myself that this time would be different. Nobody could have gotten here any quicker than I did, I had a chance to do some good this time around. I had the ability to affect the outcome of things, I wasn't some scarred eighteen-year-old soldier anymore with everything around him out of control. I had the power to stop this shit.

I kept repeating this to myself until a tall and lovely woman with dark hair and bright, hazel-colored eyes answered my knock at the door.

She'd barely opened it, when a man's voice, somewhere behind her said, "Honey, have you got that?"

"Yes, Jimmy, I've got the door," she said, over her shoulder, a lilt in her voice that was as appealing as her deep hazel eyes.

"I'm Matt," I told her. "Matt Rossiter. I'm an old friend of Smitty's from the Army."

She smiled and opened the door wide for me. "Come in. My husband's mentioned you a number of times. I'm sure he'll be happy to see you."

I stepped inside, wondering how Smitty had ended up with such a beauty.

"Thanks," I told her as she closed the door behind me.

I took in the small living-room at a glance: sparsely furnished, it had old, cream-colored, plaster walls, a threadbare, brown carpet, and a large, old-fashioned, oak desk that took up all the space at one end of the room. Between the size of the desk, and the big, heavy bookcases that lined the walls on either side of it, the room looked seriously out of balance – like if you walked over there, that whole end of the living-room would tip down to the ground while the other end rose up in the air.

"Matt! I'll be damned."

It was Smitty, coming out from what I took to be the kitchen, a can of Pepsi in his left hand, while his right propelled his wheelchair at a good clip. He looked like he'd hardly aged a day, except for his hair going gray – had one of those chubby faces that seemed to defy age.

"Smitty." I met him halfway across the room and shook his hand. He had a big smile on his face.

"Man, what a blast from the past," he said, continuing to pump my hand. "I didn't know if you were alive or dead. It's good to see you again."

"Same-same," I told him, trying not to stare at the stumps of his legs.

"Matt, this is my wife, Nora."

"Glad to meet you – I'd love to stay and chat, but I've got to go," she said.

"She's just on her way out to make deliveries," Smitty told me.

"Deliveries?" I asked.

"Yeah," he said. "I make Biscotti. Right here in our own kitchen. We've got six different varieties."

"You?" I said. "You're talking about those cookie type things that are hard as rocks?"

Nora laughed. "You don't want to eat them like a normal cookie, Matt."

"You dunk them," Smitty told me. "You know, with a latte or a mocha or any kind of coffee drink."

"Oh, I get it," I said. I wasn't a fancy coffee drinker – liked mine straight-up out of my Mr. Coffee. "Got to admit, I almost broke a tooth on the first and last Biscotti I tried."

Both Smitty and his wife smiled. "You'll have to fix him a latte while he's here," she told him. "Have him try one of your Biscotti's with it."

"So," I said to her, trying to make small talk before I got down to serious business with Smitty. "You're off making deliveries, huh?"

"Yes," she told me. "Seaside to Cannon Beach and a few spots in between."

"We've got fifteen different accounts now," Smitty said proudly.

"Sixteen," his wife corrected him.

"That's right. You just got Lombardi's Espresso, didn't you?" He turned to me, saying, "Never argue with the sales department, Matt. I'm just the baker."

"You're right," his wife said, giving him a playful pat on the arm, then a quick peck on the lips. "I do have to be going," she told me. "It usually takes me about three hours round trip. Will you be here when I get back?" she asked me. "You'd be more than welcome to share a meal with us."

"She cooks a mean lasagna," Smitty told me.

"Thanks," I said. "But I don't think so – I'll have to be getting back to Seattle by then."

Nora gave me a warm smile. "Well, the invitation's still open if you are here." She offered me her hand, saying, "It was really nice to meet you, Matt."

"Likewise," I told her, noticing that she had incredibly smooth hands.

She went to the front door, then paused and asked me, "By the way, what do you do for a living, Matt?"

"I'm a private investigator."

"Oh," she said. After a long moment, she added, "That's interesting," then left.

"You sure have a lovely wife," I told Smitty.

"I'm a lucky guy," he said. "But you – a PI – really?"

"Yup."

"How about that," he said. "I'm a part-time baker and you're a PI. Who knows what people end up doing after the war? Sit down; take a load off, Matt."

I took a seat on the fat brown recliner next to him.

"I'm a writer, too, you know," he told me.

"Really?"

"I'm not published yet or anything, but I'm working on it."

"What do you write?"

"I just finished a memoir. Memoir about my time in Nam. Got it right here," he said, rolling over to the big oak desk and picking up a thick stack of paper.

"That's nice," I said, thinking that nothing about Nam was nice.

"Actually," said Smitty, rolling up in front of me in his wheelchair, "I've been looking for somebody to read it over – somebody who was there, like you, Matt – somebody to tell me if I got everything right about Nam. My memories kind of blur about some stuff."

He seemed really happy about his manuscript. I didn't want to spoil it for him, but I needed to get down to business. "Smitty," I said, "somebody's trying to— "

"Oh, it's not all blood and guts and angst," he went on. "We had some good times over there, too, didn't— "

"Smitty," I repeated firmly. "Somebody's trying— "

"Yeah," he smiled at whatever-the-hell good times he was talking about. "I got it all in there, good and bad and— "

I reached out and grabbed his wrist to get his attention. "Smitty, listen up!" I told him. "Somebody's trying to kill us. Everybody from our old squad. I think you're a target, man."

"What?" He stammered a bit, like what I said just didn't compute. "What? What did you say?"

"Somebody's going to try and kill you," I repeated. "You're next on the list."

"What list? What are you talking about?"

I showed him the copy of our squad list.

"Damn, look at that," he said, setting his manuscript down in his lap and running a finger over the list. "I forgot about some of these guys. These names really help. Can I— "

"Fuck that!" I said, standing up. "You don't get it, man. Some asshole is using that list to kill us all off. All in order. Started with Rivers, then Baker, then me, then almost got Shabazz, and you're next."

He looked up at me, his eyes finally showing that he got the message. I didn't know how he could be so happy-go-lucky in his condition, let alone write about the shit we went through, but he finally got my message.

"No shit?" he asked quietly. "You mean— "

"Yeah. That's how it is."

I sat back down and gave him the short version of the story, start to finish. When I was done, I asked him if he could think of anybody – anybody at all – who could have a bad enough case-of-the-ass to be doing this.

Smitty shook his head 'no.'

"You sure?"

"Well," he said at length, "now that you mention it, I'd say with that bastard Rivers dead, there's only one person who might fit the bill."

"Who?"

"Corporal Maloney," said Smitty, running his finger down the platoon list and stabbing it at Maloney's name. "Rivers' asshole flunky. He was Rivers' enforcer, remember? Only troop I ever met who was as badass as that prick."

"Yeah." I took the list back from him – stared at the corporal's name for a second, his brown-nosing, evil face seeming to jump out at me. "I've thought about him, too, Smitty. You could be right. I don't know where he's living yet, but I will be paying him a visit when I find out."

Smitty was quiet for minute, then said, "I sure can't think of anyone else. But even if it's him, why? It's been almost thirty years since we were there. Why would he be doing this? Why now?"

"That's the big question," I told him. "You're right in asking why. Getting the motive usually narrows down the list of suspects."

"Do you have any suspects, Matt? I mean other than the corporal?"

"No. All I know for sure is, it has to be somebody who was over there with us."

"Great," he said. "So, it's all out of control, huh? Just like the fucking war." He paused, frowned, and shook his head. "Well, I'm not going back to that."

"What do you mean?"

"It is what it is," said Smitty, stoic, but then adding an inexplicable smile. "I've got a good life and a wonderful wife. I'm not going to let this get me down."

"What are you going to do?"

"What *can* I do?" he asked in return. "I was down for too long with a bunch of what-if's: what if this, what if that? It's bullshit. You got what you got, and you make the best of it. If you're down, you get back up on your feet." He paused, then laughed ruefully. "Even if you haven't got any feet."

"You've got to do *something*, man," I told him. "The Smitty I knew never talked like this. Hell, trouble came up, you were one of the first to jump to."

"Yeah, well, I'm not so good at jumping anymore."

"Dammit! This guy's a stone-cold killer."

"Fuck! What do you want?" he fairly yelled. "I don't think you're going to stick around here and baby-sit me forever. I can protect myself if I have to."

"Smitty," I said, not wanting to say it, but saying it anyway. "How are you going to do that? You're stuck in that chair."

"I've got a shotgun," he said. "And I can get around if I need to. I've got prosthetics – couple artificial legs – I walk with them pretty good, even though they hurt."

"I'm glad," I said, "but— "

"They hurt like hell, actually," he went on. "They hurt like a sonofabitch, to tell the truth. I put them on every day and walk around for a while anyway. Until I can hardly stand it anymore. And you know why?"

"No."

"Because they make me really appreciate my wheelchair – how nice it is – how good it feels to sit in it. How lucky I am to have it. Nam's over man, I don't live in the past. I make the most out of what I've got."

"I can understand what you're saying, but— "

"Here," he said, handing me his manuscript. "That's the past. It's all in there. If you really want to help me, you'll take it and read it and let me know what you think. Will you do that for me?"

"Sure," I said, really not wanting to read what replayed in my head every day.

"Thanks," said Smitty. "Writing that was the best thing I ever did. Counselor told me that writing and talking about it was the best way to expunge that crap. Or at least come to grips with it. It's true. You know, I used to drink like a fish. Now I don't touch the stuff – don't need it – haven't had a drink in over ten years."

"Good for you," I said, thinking about the bottle of Wild Turkey I'd picked up on my way to Smitty's. "That's a real accomplishment."

"So, Matt," he said. "You want to have some coffee with me? Try some of my biscotti?"

"Thanks, but I better get going. I've got a long drive back to Seattle." I stood up; the heavy manuscript in my hands, knowing there wasn't anything else I could do for him. I'd warned him, seen some of the old Smitty return when I got a rise out of him, but he still kept acting like everything was just peachy.

"You'll call me when you've read it, won't you?" Smitty asked as he followed me to the door.

"Sure, I will."

He reached up to shake hands with me, then pulled me down to his level and put a vise-like hug on me. "Thanks, man," he said. "Thanks for everything."

I told him to tell his wife goodbye for me, then went out the door, and got into my car. I tossed the manuscript on the passenger seat, looked at it for a long moment, and didn't know if I'd ever get around to reading it.

In the meantime, I hit the Wild Turkey. I was still tired, was frustrated, decided to stay put for a while and pull a little guard duty on Smitty. He was happy as a lark, but I knew somebody was coming for him. So, I wiled away the time, attuned to any danger between pulls on the Wild Turkey that always made me feel better.

Yeah, Matt, I told myself, guard duty's a bitch. Most of the time, nothing but nothing happens, but you're on edge every second, and you're always tired, that's just the way it is. You can't doze off – too many people depend on you.

The Wild Turkey's settling you down and you're comfortable and relaxed and don't give a fuck if your eyes are getting heavy…

…and it's my first time alone on guard duty. It's just a dream, I keep telling myself – you've had it before – but there I am. It's like a movie: I see myself manning the machine gun, see the sandbags my M-60 is resting on – but I also see what I'm seeing beyond the gun – the dark; the half-moon that casts an eerie glow to the hundred yards of clearing between me and the tree line; the stillness, the absolute quiet where the loudest sound is my own heart beating; the fear, so strong it's like a taste in my mouth.

I've only been in-country for a week. I've been scared for the whole time, but I can't let it show, can't let the other guys know. I keep thinking that I could die at any moment, and what's it all worth? Humping it through the jungle; filling sandbags and endlessly digging foxholes. Trying to talk to the other guys when they will hardly talk to me. Trying to fight the sticky heat with a drink of water that's warm and tastes strongly of my plastic canteen. Worrying about land mines, trip-wires, punji-pits, ambushes, snakes, scorpions, and the overwhelming fatigue.

I'm tired all the time – never enough sleep – like now. I rest my head against a sandbag. Sleep calls to me – invites me in – says that everything will be fine, you just need to rest…

…and there's movement in front of me!

It's a swirl of mist by the tree line. It's nothing. The mist slowly roils toward me like a wall of thick fog. On it comes, yard by yard, until it's only about a hundred feet away.

Something's in the mist! A dark shape…

...and my fingers on the trigger...
...but I freeze when the dark shape comes into focus...
...it's a man! An NVA soldier, his assault rifle at the ready...
...and on he comes...
...don't think he sees me...
...I should shoot...
...but it's just a dream...
...the mist begins to wash over me...
...he's only ten yards away...
...I squeeze off a long burst...
...he virtually disintegrates as the heavy rounds tear into him...
...his blood spits and spatters...becomes part of the mist around him...
...and all up and down the line, everybody opens up...
...streams of red tracers shooting into the clearing...
...but there's no return fire...
He died and I didn't.
I feel better.
...it was just a dream...

I jerk fully awake. I'm still outside Smitty's place, only there's nobody to shoot to make me feel any better.

I glance at my watch – it's been several hours since I got into the car. I must have dozed off. This guard duty's a bust. I'm drenched in sweat, but a little less tired. Hell, anybody could have walked by me while I was dreaming. I panic thinking about it and start to bail out of the car, then see Smitty's wife going up to the house. The front door's open and Smitty's greeting her at the door. Everything's fine, I didn't drop the ball.

Get it together, man. You can't do any more. It's a long drive back to Seattle and you need to figure out where you're going to spend the night. Whatever bastard is trying to kill us off will make a mistake somewhere along the way and you'll be waiting for him. There's no giving up once you've started. If it's hard, you've got to be harder.

I pointed the nose of my Mustang up the steep hill from Smitty's, got the air conditioning running, and took another long pull off the Wild Turkey. I could only hope that he'd be OK. Smitty was pink-clouding it, I was sure. He was pink-clouding it over the danger, not alcohol, but it was same-same. I remember when I first heard that term. Four days into A.A., one of the guys told me that I was pink-clouding it: "You've only stopped drinking and doing drugs for four days, man," he told me. "But you say everything's fine. No problem. That's what we call pink-clouding it, Matt. You can't pretend everything's good when you know it's not. You've got to work the program. Read the Big Book. Stick with it. It might get worse before it gets better, but it does get better."

He was right. It did get better. I stayed off the dope and just enjoyed my Wild Turkey.

Chapter Eighteen

I decided to drive back to Seattle on the Washington side of the river. The Mustang's V-8 rumbled as I drove up the steep onramp to the monster bridge that crossed the mouth of the wide Columbia. It was an old bridge, all green painted steel girders and trusses that stretched out ahead of me for miles. I'd never driven the thing before and was surprised at how tall the high-rise portion of it was on the Astoria side. It seemed to be hundreds of feet down to the water. Reminded me of the abyss that some old German author was always talking about in this novel we studied in my first year of college.

Damned if I could remember his name, though, much less the title of the book. That was par for the course, because I was stoned most of the time and never finished the class. I did remember about the abyss – how he stared into it and found it inviting, like it was beckoning him all the time, and how welcome it would be to just give up and enter into it.

I suddenly felt very small, tiny as could be, imagined falling forever and ever, and the peace it would bring as the mighty river swallowed me.

I gunned the Mustang! Floored it – was doing seventy as I dropped down from the high-rise, the green girders and river whizzing by in a blur. Hit eighty or more a couple times flying along the rest of the two-lane bridge that seemed to stretch on into infinity. Passed cars like they were stuck in first gear, dodged a few oncoming cars and trucks by a whisker, and made the remaining miles to the other side in two minutes flat.

I felt fully alive when I reached the Washington side. Felt like I did that time in Nam when a bullet went through my helmet and creased my skull. I had a concussion and needed a bunch of stitches, They put me in a Huey and Medi-vaced me to the hospital in Bien Hoa. A fat shot of Morphine that made me dream of pretty nurses and air conditioning and cool, crisp sheets and endless sleep. The thrumming chopper reminded me of Ravi Shankar's sitar music and the flight was all surreal and floating and psychedelic like the Beatle's Magical Mystery Tour. The medic on board kept telling me it was probably just a bad concussion, don't worry, you'll be back on your feet in no time.

I said, "No worries, man, it's all beautiful. I'm alive! I'm alive!"

I turned the Mustang in at the Seattle/Tacoma airport, picked up my Firebird from the parking garage, and headed for Jessica Ito's condo.

• • •

Jessica's voice came over the intercom. "Matt?"

"I need you Jessica," I said.

"For a guy who needs me, you've sure been gone a lot."

"I do need you," I said.

"I haven't seen or heard from you," she told me. "No way to reach you or anything."

"I'm here now."

There was silence for a moment, then the door buzzed and clicked, allowing me entrance.

I took the elevator up – found Jessica waiting for me outside her open door in the hallway. She must have just gotten out of the shower, because she had a white towel wrapped like a turban around her head, and wore a short, white terrycloth robe loosely cinched at her narrow waist. The tiniest trickle of water ran down her swan-like neck to the top of her exposed cleavage, which was deliciously sexy. She was one of those women, like Grace, who defied age – didn't need lipstick or any other makeup – just was her glowing, glistening, gorgeous self.

Expecting her to give me another ration of shit, I was surprised when she just took me by the hand and led me into her living room without another word. I didn't say anything either – there was nothing to say – the situation spoke for itself as she came close to me and tenderly stroked the back of my hand, then with the lightest touch, worked her way up to the hairs on my wrist.

"I was so worried about you," she finally said, her body scented with the lilac soap she had always been fond of. "I thought— "

"Don't think," I told her. "I'm here, you're here, that's all we need."

The lawyer in her told her to object, but she didn't, just said, "Matt, there's something you need to know. The judge ruled on the Benny Luc trial yesterday."

"Already?" I asked. "That was quick. He must have known the bastard was guilty all along."

"No, Matt. There wasn't any guilty or not guilty," she said. "The judge declared a mistrial."

"What?"

"Defense asked for a mistrial, and the judge agreed."

"What the hell? He just said there wouldn't be a— "

"He didn't believe your testimony, Matt." She looked deeply into my eyes. "He thought you lied."

I didn't say anything.

She put a hand on my shoulder and said, "You could be facing a charge of perjury. Maybe not, though, it's awfully difficult to prove."

Again, there was nothing to say.

"Matt," she said, putting both hands firmly on my shoulders and pressing her body against mine, like that was the best way to get my attention. "Benny Luc's been released. You know he's going to come after you."

"Who isn't?" I asked, then pulled her robe open and kissed her.

I left before Jessica woke up the next morning. I couldn't sleep for shit. Jessica, on the other hand, slept like a baby. She was blissful and beautiful, only partially covered by her silk sheets, when I quietly went out the door. I didn't leave a note – didn't know what to say, especially since she'd wanted us to have breakfast at The Athenian in the Public Market this morning. We'd have a romantic breakfast some other day. I'd even bring her flowers.

The seagulls were swirling and keening at the nearby waterfront, where I got a cup of coffee and sat on a bench watching the sparkling waters of Elliott Bay. I needed to talk to Rachel, fill her in on what had happened with Shabazz and my visit with Smitty, see if she'd dug up any other info that could help my case.

I drove up to her place on Capitol Hill, hoping I could catch her at home. On the way, I got another cup of coffee at a drive-thru espresso stand – went for a latte, which I hardly ever drank, with plenty of extra everything in it. I needed the sugar boost, and enough caffeine to start the day, I soon pulled up outside Rachel's place.

I was surprised to hear loud music coming from her house. Very loud music – Neil Young's 'Cinnamon Girl' – just rocking out. It wasn't Rachel's sort of music; she preferred the mellow stuff and never seemed the type to blow out her speakers. I knocked on the door. Had to knock again even louder.

When the door finally opened, I said, "Rachel, I – "

"Hey, Matt." It was Boo, not Rachel standing in the doorway.

"Whoa," I said. "What are you doing here? Where's Rachel?"

"Nice to see you too," he said, then laughed. "She's out and about. I don't know where exactly. Come on in, dude. Where you been?"

"I just got back from Astoria."

"Oh yeah, Astoria," Boo said, laying back into a big overstuffed armchair and motioning me to take a seat on the white couch across from him. "Right – that's where she went – Astoria."

"Astoria? What's she doing in Astoria?"

"Went down to find an old girlfriend of mine."

"Who's that?"

"Some case she's working on, man. Astoria must be one happening place," said Boo, so mellow you'd think he'd just melt into his armchair. It was obvious he was stoned. Of course, Boo was an original stoner, so it would've been unusual to find him otherwise, even at 9:00 am. He was used to it. Called Mary Jane his fuel.

Boo got all quiet. Turned on a dime from happy talk to no talk. I'd been around

Boo long enough to know that something was up. Something not good. Something very serious when he did the Jekyll & Hyde.

"You were right, dude," he told me.

"About what?"

"You asked me what I'm doing here at Rachel's – I came down to help you."

"What do you mean?"

"The warning you gave me. I blew you off, but you were right. Some shithead shot at us – a couple shots, actually."

"What? Where?" I asked, sitting bolt upright on the couch. "When?"

"Yesterday." Boo told me. "My place in Bellingham. We'd just gone out to the car when this shitbird opened up on us."

"Us? You and Rachel?"

"Yeah. She came up to see me about my old girlfriend. Anyway, we hit the dirt at the first shot. I pulled her under my Blazer at the next shot. Got my gun out of the glove-box, but the bastard was gone by the time I was ready for him."

"But Rachel was OK?"

"What did I just say?" he told me. "Anyway, I found two shell casings. Came from a Big-boy gun – 10mm."

"You see who did it?"

"Happened too fast, man. I should've known the shit was on when I heard the music.

"What music?"

"Came from this black BMW across the street when we first went outside. Real loud, blaring Hendrix song: 'Machine Gun.' Then the shooting started.

"Sounds like my guy." I didn't like Rachel being exposed to this crap – wondered if I should have involved her in the first place – never thought she'd be in the line of fire just trying to find the troops from my squad.

"There's something else you need to know," Boo told me.

"What's that?"

"Smitty's dead."

"Say *wha*t?" The words hit me like a punch in the gut. "Can't be. I just saw him."

"Killed. Like in murdered, you know," said Boo. "Rachel found him. Said somebody tried to make it look like a suicide, but she knew better. There was Hendrix music playing in his house when she got there – kept playing over and over she said. Gotta be our guy who did it."

"Shit!" I stood up. "Why didn't you tell me sooner?"

"Hey," said Boo, also rising to his feet. "What's the difference if I told you about Smitty first, or about the asshole trying to kill me and Rachel? Same-same, dude. There is some good news, though."

"Like what?"

"Like Rachel found some info on Corporal Maloney. He's got a P.O. Box in Sultan. He's living somewhere up there, dude. My money's on him, little mini-Rivers asshole that he was. He's the only one mean enough to be doing all this shit."

"Yeah. The only one left from the squad who hasn't been killed or had an attempt made on his life," I said, thinking about how often Corporal Maloney accompanied Rivers in my dreams, and also feeling sorry-assed because poor Smitty was dead and I hadn't even taken the time to look at his memoir that he so wanted me to read.

"No worries," said Boo, his jaw so tight he was speaking through his teeth. "I'm with you this point on. I got an arsenal in my duffle bag. AR-15's, Glocks, you name it." Then he smiled – the same crazy-ass-smile that he always got when we were on ambush-patrol. "This dude wants war, he *gets* war."

Chapter Nineteen

My cellphone rang just as Boo and I were ready to take off. It was Tanaka.

"Dale," I said. "How'd you get my number?"

"Not from you!" Tanaka yelled. "I got it from that PI you trained, Rachel Stern. Why the hell haven't you kept in touch with me?"

"Lots of shit's been going on, I— "

"It's a lot of shit all right! You're maybe facing perjury, and Benny Luc's on the loose thanks to you. That's just for starters! I've got everybody else up my ass about this shit. The Chief, the Renton Chief, and the D.E.A, the F.B.I., and now the A.T.F. about Rivers, for God's sake! What have you been doing? They all want to talk to you, Matt."

"Fine," I said. "Calm down – I'll talk to them."

"When?"

"Later," I said, then hung up.

The phone rang twice more in short order. I didn't answer it.

We needed an operating base, so Boo and I got a room at a motel down on Eastlake Boulevard, near where my houseboat used to be. Got all our gear ready, then we hit the road to Sultan, both pretty pumped. All we had to go on was the PO Box Corporal Maloney used there, but Sultan was barley a pinprick on the map, and I figured it wouldn't be hard to find him in such a small place.

It wasn't that long a drive. We'd take Highway 2 into Monroe, then follow it east up the Skykomish River in the direction of Stevens Pass. About an hour drive at most. As we passed the complex of penitentiaries commonly known as the Monroe Reformatory, I said, "Any luck, that's going to be Maloney's new home."

"If the sonofabitch is still alive when I get through with him," Boo told me. The town of Sultan fronted Hwy. 2, with the Skykomish River on the right, and what there was of Sultan on the left as you drove east. The business district, if you could call it that, was all of a couple blocks long, and consisted of a small bakery, a sub sandwich shop, a burger joint, and a few other small establishments. The town didn't even have a single stoplight. I assumed the rest of it must be located behind the tiny business area, and it turned out I was right.

We took a left off the highway near where the Sultan River emptied into the much larger Skykomish River. We passed a small bank and a tavern, then came to the Post Office.

"Where should we start?" asked Boo.

"We'll ask around – show his picture, see if anybody's seen him."

"His picture? You've got a photo of him?"

"Yeah," I said. "Of sorts."

"What's that supposed to mean?"

I pulled over and parked just down from the Post Office. Then I reached into the back seat and grabbed Smitty's memoir – I had placed the photo of our old squad inside it. I took it out and handed it to Boo.

"Hell, that's us in Nam!" he said with a big smile. "The whole squad. Cool. Where'd you get this?"

"Rivers had it. Had all sorts of shit from the war. Even kept the ears he took."

"Sounds like him," said Boo. He poked a finger onto the photo. "There that sorry fuck is, right there, dude. Rivers, what a piece of work." I turned off the ignition and unbuckled my seatbelt. "Look at you," Boo told me. "Skinny as a rail, and still wet-behind-the-ears. What were you: eighteen?"

"Yeah." I glanced at the photo again, and couldn't help noticing the difference between Boo and me back then. I looked like a kid, while he was all snarly-faced, crazy-eyed, Rambo-like. No wonder Rivers never fucked with him.

"And Magic," said Boo. "Look at that big 'fro he grew. It's a wonder he could get his helmet over it." Boo laughed, then continued. "Hard to believe some of these guys are gone. I mean, like sure, enough time's passed that you expect people might have died, but murdered...that's cold. There's the fuck that must have done 'em all. Corporal Maloney himself. Horse-faced jerk-off!"

"Probably so," I said. "Let's go find him."

"Just a second," Boo told me, eyeing the memoir I still held. "What's that big binder you pulled this photograph out of? Got more pictures in it?"

"Smitty's memoir," I told him. "Bunch of shit about the war."

"He's an author? Who'd of thought?"

"Not yet," I said. "I think he wanted to publish it."

"What's he say about me?"

"Says you're a stoned-out wild man."

"He's got that right."

"I actually don't know what he said about you, Boo. I've hardly looked at it. It was important to him, and now he's dead. I just couldn't handle reading it yet."

"Don't sweat it, man. We'll make Smitty proud." He pointed at himself, saying, "All we've gotta do is go wild on the Corporal."

I kept the photo with me, and tossed the memoir into the rear seat. We got out of the car.

First place we hit was the tavern. Place called The Hitching Post – old, false-fronted building like it was out of the Wild West – all knotty-pine paneled inside, dark and cool with the air conditioning running. Had a lit-up juke box playing country music.

Even though it was before lunch, there were three folks bellied up to the bar, already drinking schooners. The bartender, big man, fortyish, with a salt & pepper beard, wearing a blue denim work shirt, nodded as we approached him.

"Morning," he said. "What'll it be?"

"Shot of Wild Turkey, straight up," I told him.

"Only beer and wine. No Class H license," the guy told me. "Sorry."

"That's OK," I said. "We really came in just trying to find somebody."

"Oh, yeah?" He gave me a look, not really suspicious, but not overly friendly either. "Like who?"

I pulled out the photo and pointed to the Corporal. "This guy," I said. "'Course, he's about thirty years older now. Heard he was living here in Sultan. You recognize him? His name's Maloney."

"Maloney," said the bartender, then gave the photo a second look. "Yeah, that's Crazy Mike all right."

"Crazy Mike?" I asked.

"Yeah, that's what everybody calls him. Wouldn't have recognized him without the name, though. Lot heavier now."

"Have you seen him lately?"

"Not lately. He's been 86'd out of here since last year."

"Why's that?"

"He's crazy, that's why. PTSD. Too many fights. Crazy Vietnam vet, you know the type."

Boo got his back up at that remark. "No, I don't know the type." His own crazy smile started to cross his lips, but I tapped him on the arm to hold it steady, and asked the bartender, "You know where he lives?"

"Nope. People say he camps out in the woods somewhere."

"Hey Bill," an old man at the other end of the bar called out. "How about another schooner, huh?"

"Coming up, Jimmy," said the bartender, then briefly turned back to us. "Well, I got to get back to work. Good luck with Crazy Mike if you do find him."

"Yeah," said the old man, evidently having overheard our conversation. "Good luck is right."

"Sounds like you know him," I said taking a few steps toward the guy. "Do you know where he's at?"

"Don't know and don't want to know," he told me as Bill the bartender filled up a new schooner for him. "He's a real asshole."

"You got that right, Jimmy," said the guy wearing a plaid shirt on the other side of the old man. He laughed, raised his schooner to the old man, and sarcastically said, "Here's to Crazy Mike!" Then they both laughed and toasted each other.

"Let's di-di," Boo told me. "We're not going to find him in here."

Even though it was still pretty hot when we left, the air outside the Hitching Post seemed crisp and clean after the booze-scented mustiness of the tavern.

"Well that was a bust," said Boo.

"Not really," I told him. "We found out he lives in the woods at least."

"Look around, dude," he said, gesturing with his hands. "It's all forest up here. Take an army to search it."

"What, you're giving up?"

"Fuck no. You know me when I'm pissed."

"Fine. Let's keep asking around," I said. "How about the bank? He might have a disability rating from the VA for his PTSD. He'd have to cash his disability checks somewhere. They might know something."

We walked to the nearby bank, but of course it was closed on Sunday.

The Post Office was the next building up, had to be where Maloney had his P.O. Box, it was closed as well. So, we went back the car and drove toward the main drag, intending to hit the sub sandwich place, the burger stand, and the other small businesses we had passed as we came into Sultan.

As we passed a small side street just before the main highway, Boo said, "Hold it! Stop and back up."

"Why?" I asked, slowing and coming to a stop.

"Down the street we just went by," he said. "We should check it out."

I still didn't know what he was talking about, but looked in my rearview for any traffic behind us, then put it in reverse and slowly backed up the car.

Check it," Boo told me as we came to a stop parallel to the side street. "Look to your left," he told me, pointing down the small street. "See that little white building half a block away? Got a flagpole with an American flag on it. Didn't notice it before. What is it?"

We found out in short order. It was a small American Legion Hall with a big gravel parking lot around it.

"Oh, well," said Boo. "It's probably not open either."

"Don't know about that," I told him, looking at the old, shingle-sided building about the size of a single-wide mobile home. "Shouldn't be flying the flag if they're closed over the weekend."

"Be a waste of time," Boo told me. "I mean, how many Vietnam vets do you know who joined the Legion or the VFW? Just a bunch old farts who don't like us in those places. All they ever care about is W.W.II or Korea."

I knew he was right, but parked in the gravel lot, off to the side of the building, anyway. We saw the front entrance door open up, and a tall man about my age stepped onto the front porch, looked around for a moment. He didn't seem to notice us, then went back inside, leaving the door open.

"Let's go talk to him," I told Boo.

"Whatever."

We made for the open doors, the dusty pea-gravel crunching beneath our feet. Almost at the doorway, I heard a rumbling behind us. It grew into a roar as Boo and turned around and saw twenty or more bikers coming toward us, the unmistakable grumble of their motorcycles identifying them as big Harley Davidsons. Most of them were choppers – low slung, elongated bikes that had extra-wide rear wheels, some with chrome chicken-bars behind their seats, and many with ridiculously tall handlebars.

"Here comes trouble," said Boo. He smiled wickedly, and reached under his bright Hawaiian shirt for the Glock he kept holstered at the small of his back.

"Stay cool," I told him. The bikers came to a stop in front of us, fanning out some as they did so. The closest two, both bearded, wore black-painted Nazi-style military helmets. The rest wore helmets of various styles, while a couple had no helmets at all. Every one of them had saddle-bags on their bikes that seemed to be overstuffed. A few of the bikes were equipped with side-cars, but instead of carrying passengers, they were loaded high, covered with blue tarps secured with long bungee-cords. Half of them shut their engines off, but those nearest us menacingly throttled their bikes up and down, as if to show us they were the top dogs here.

"I don't think this Gilligan's Island joker likes us," said the biker with the Nazi-helmet, referring to Boo's yellow Hawaiian shirt and the hand he'd kept behind it.

"Think you're right, Harley," the similarly helmeted guy beside him agreed.

"Your name's really Harley?" I asked the biker who kept staring at Boo.

"Yeah." He put the kickstand down on his bike and stepped off of it. He was big – bigger than big – had to be three-hundred pounds or more. "What of it?" he asked, coming toward me.

Chapter Twenty

I was getting ready for anything, when another biker drove past the big man and stopped beside me. This one had an eight-foot trailer attached to the end of his tricycle-style bike that was also full of stuff covered with a tied-down tarp. A woman in black leather rode with him, her arms wrapped around his waist, her backside snug against the bike's chicken-bar. They both wore shiny, rounded blue helmets, with dark tinted visors. As they put the visors up and removed their helmets, I recognized Billy and Sheri who I'd met a Rivers' house.

"Take it easy, Harley," Billy told the big man. "This is Matt Rossiter. The Nam vet with that built '67 Firebird I told you about. He's cool."

Harley looked over his shoulder to where I'd parked my car. "Yeah, I saw it riding in. That's yours, huh?" he asked me. "Sweet." Then he turned his attention back to Boo. "But who's this other old dude? He don't seem cool at all."

"He is," I told Harley. "He's with me." I turned to Boo. "Say hello, Boo."

"Hello," Boo told him, his expression unchanged.

"Hello yourself, Matt Rossiter," Sheri said to me, stepping off of Billy's chopper. "I didn't think I'd see you again."

I smiled and said hello in return, thinking she looked a lot better than the first time I'd seen her, especially now wearing form-fitting black leather. I didn't want Billy getting the wrong impression though.

"What are you doing here?" I asked him.

"Could ask you the same," he said.

"We're just trying to look up a guy from our old squad," I told him. "You?"

"Toys for Tots."

"Toys for Tots?"

"Yeah," he said. "This is our annual run. We're all loaded up with toys we've been collecting. Drop them here at the American Legion, then it's up over the pass to Wenatchee and pick up another load, then we're off to Cle Elum, and back over Snoqualmie Pass to Seattle."

"No shit?" I said. "That's nice."

"Always support the troops," Billy told me. "Marines have done Toys for Tots for years, and we always help them."

"What are you packing?" Harley asked Boo.

"Glock .40."

"Good gun," said Harley. He opened his motorcycle jacket, which exposed the pistol he carried on his belt. "Mine's a 9 mm. Beretta. Got comfortable with it in Iraq."

"You're a vet, too, huh?" Boo asked him.

"Desert Storm," Harley said proudly. "We shouldn't have stopped, though. Should've gone all the way."

"Same with Nam," said Boo. "We should've gone all the way."

Harley smiled. "You're OK, man. We oughta get a beer."

"After we unload," Billy told Harley, loud enough for everybody to hear, then asked me, "You up for some beers?"

"Hell yes!" said a number of the other bikers closest to us. "Suds are good!"

"Why not?" I told Billy.

As if on cue, the guy with the American Legion came out. "Hi fellas," he said. "You can pack it all in. Just put it off to the side of the meeting room."

"Let's get to it!" Billy yelled.

Each of the bikers grabbed their saddlebags and headed to the Legion Hall with them. All except two of them, who had gone over to my Firebird and were grinning as they appraised it. The one standing near the trunk was skinny as hell, and wore old fashioned, tight fitting, brown leather headgear like pilots used in WWII. He waved and caught my eye, then animatedly nodded his head up and down for my benefit, sharing his appreciation of my vintage muscle car.

"Yo, BJ and Slick!" Billy yelled at them. "That means you, too! Let's get this stuff inside."

The two men jumped to it. Went to their bikes and joined the others bringing their stuffed saddlebags into the Legion Hall.

Billy and Sheri took the bungee-cords off of the load in the small trailer. Boo and I pulled the tarp off, and were pretty amazed at the quantity and assortment of toys that it carried: used toys and new toys still in their boxes; stuffed animals; a large train set; all sorts of video games; even a couple new Nintendo machines; etc, etc. We lent a hand carrying it all in.

"Thanks for the help," Billy told me, his arms holding a load of toys that stretched clear up to his chin.

"Why not? Good cause," Boo told him, holding a rather precarious stack of toys in his own arms. "Besides, a beer sounds good. Too damned hot out here."

Took a while, but we got the last stuff out of the trailer and inside with the help of Harley and some of the other bikers. There were so many toys that they filled up half the side wall area of the place, which was really just one long, softwood-floored room, with a kitchen area in back, and the American and Washington State flags posted by a podium at the far end.

I also took note of the back of Billy's jacket while we got the toys squared away. His jacket had sported a biker patch that read 'Desperados' when I'd first met him at Rivers' house the other day. He'd changed the patch; it now read 'Outlaws' – a much bigger and way more notorious biker gang – had the gang's logo, a white skull on a black background. I'd have to ask about that when we had our beer together.

We'd just finished up, Boo and I and Billy and Sheri, with the last of the stuff, when the guy in charge of the Hall shook Billy's hand and told him thanks.

"No sweat, Frank," said Billy. "We'll be back next weekend with more. Our Bellingham Chapter's got other business, so we're going to do that run for them."

"Great," Frank told him. "Thanks to you guys, too," he told Boo and me.

"So," Billy said to me. "You know where the Hitching Post tavern's at?"

"Yeah."

"Good. Meet you there." As he walked out with Sheri, she looked over her shoulder and gave me a sexy look that I hoped she wouldn't repeat.

I took out our old squad's photo, and showed it to Frank. "You ever see this guy around here?" I asked, pointing out Corporal Maloney.

"Can't say as I have," Frank said, peering at the photo over the top of the glasses he wore. "What's this from? Vietnam?"

"Yeah; late 1968," I said. "He's heavier now. His name's Mike Maloney."

Frank almost jerked his head back from the photo, saying, "Oh, hell, him! Yeah, I've seen him. Not for a long time, though. Our Legion Post has a protection order against him. What the hell do you want with that idiot?"

"Just trying to find him. We were in the same squad together," I said. "We heard he was living in the woods somewhere up here."

"Good place for him – away from normal people," said Frank. "Check the other side of the river, to the right, across the bridge. Lot of bums set up camp there just above the riverbank. But watch yourselves: man's violent, got a screw loose."

"Thanks," I told him.

"Yeah," said Boo as we left.

When we got back to the Firebird, Boo asked, "We going right after Maloney or get that beer first?"

"Let's make it a quick drink, then get to it." I said. "Besides, I want to ask Billy about something."

"When you told me about running into him at Rivers' place, you didn't tell me he was an Outlaw."

"He wasn't one, then." I turned the engine over. "He was a Desperado."

"We'll want to be careful, dude. These bikers can be your friend one minute, then kick the shit out of you the next. The Outlaws raise all kinds of hell up in Bellingham. Newspaper said they've been trying to force the smaller clubs to join them."

"Maybe that's what happened here," I said.

We drove up the street to the Hitching Post where all the choppers were angle-parked in a neat line. We heard a lot of yelling as we went inside, which gave me an instant mental picture of a bunch of bikers tearing up the place. But that was just the cliché. In fact, they were seated around the tavern like any normal customers having a really good time – some at the bar, others at tables, a couple playing a rowdy game of darts and yelling as each outscored the other.

Harley saw Boo and said, "Come on over and join me, man!"

As Boo headed to Harley's table, Billy motioned me over to where he was sitting beside Sheri in a booth. I joined them, but before I sat down, Billy told Sheri, "Take your beer and go play darts or something, babe."

"I want to stay, Billy," she said.

"What did I say?"

She shrugged, not happy, but did as she was told.

Billy poured me a glass of beer from the pitcher on the table as I sat across from him. "So," he said. "You find out any more about who killed Jack?"

"Not really," I said, unsure of how much to tell him about Rivers.

"Too bad." Billy raised his glass. "Here's to Jack Rivers," he said. "Toughest motherfucker I ever rode with."

I clinked my glass into his, but wasn't toasting to any glowing memory of sergeant Rivers, just the fact that he was dead.

"Speaking of Rivers," I said. "When was the last time you saw him? Sheri said he'd been gone for quite a while."

Billy's eyes narrowed a bit, but he still seemed friendly enough. "He was at our clubhouse just a few weeks ago," he told me. "Jack went up to Canada on some club business. That was the last I saw of him."

"To B.C.?" I asked, thinking about what Tanaka had told me about the A.T.F. and D.E.A. tracking Rivers' involvement with guns and drugs out of British Columbia.

"Yeah," Billy told me. "Up to Vancouver. What of it?"

"Nothing," I said. "Just helps to know everything I can about somebody when I'm trying to solve a case."

Billy lit up a cigarette. "Fine. If that helps, good."

"How'd Rivers feel about you patching over?" I asked.

"Oh," he said, touching the small Outlaws patch on the front of his motorcycle jacket – same as the much larger one on the back of the jacket. "You noticed that, huh?"

"Yeah. You were a Desperado when I met you."

He leaned back and blew out a lazy smoke ring before answering. "Well Jack, he didn't like it too much. It made good sense for our business model."

"Your 'business model?' You sound like you're in high finance or something."

"I was a Business major in college," said Billy. "You know, profit & loss, cash flow, all that shit."

"I had no idea."

"Life's full of surprises, isn't it?" he told me. "Anyway, enough of that. I bet you've got some good stories about Jack in Nam. What a badass."

There was bunch of yelling behind us, and the sound of something hitting the tavern's worn wooden floor.

I jumped at the sudden noise – craned my neck around the edge of the booth, saw the two bikers who been playing darts mixing it up with each other. The bigger of the two, broad shouldered guy about thirty, had a bloody nose, but had just knocked the other guy to the floor. Less heavyset than his opponent, he picked himself right up and bull-rushed the man, which sent them both crashing to the floor. They grappled, swore, and rolled around, each trying to gain the upper hand.

"Bet Snake takes him this time," said a blonde, pony-tailed biker, seated at the table closest to the fight, with two of his friends.

"Hey!" yelled the bartender. "Break it up!"

"Let 'em fight," Billy told him, then turned to me "They're brothers – they always fight. Neither of them likes to lose." he said. "Guess that's why they always fight," he added, then laughed at his own sarcastic revelation.

"Well," I told Billy. "I'll leave you to it." I called across the way, "Hey, Boo, we gotta split!" He came over as I stood and shook hands with Billy. "We're off to find our guy. Nice seeing you again."

"Likewise," Billy told me. "Just remember – you keep me posted if you find out who wasted Jack, huh?"

"You got it."

Chapter Twenty-one

Boo and I left the Hitching Post behind, and took the bridge to the other side of the river, parking where we saw a few cars pulled over on the left of the two-lane road. The area was heavily wooded, and I could see why the Corporal would choose to make his camp somewhere around here: very private, but close access to town for supplies.

Boo and I checked our pistols when we got out of the car. We each slid a bullet into the chamber, made sure the safeties were on, then were ready to roll. We found a narrow trail that led into the forest. It paralleled the river heading west. The edges of the steep trail were overgrown with blackberry and salmonberry bushes, and overhung with the leaves of many saplings that obscured my peripheral vision as we pushed through them. With Boo on point, I found myself concentrating on his loud Hawaiian shirt as we pressed forward: nobody wore bright yellow Hawaiian shirts in Nam, so this was still Sultan, not the déjà vu that kept trying to creep up on me.

The last part of the trail was rocky as hell. I almost stumbled several times before we finally came to a small, clear area. The river was about thirty feet away to our right. The land we were on was about four feet above the riverbank itself. That's when we saw three lean-tos set back into the woods on the other side of the clearing, maybe twenty yards away. Didn't seem to be anybody around them, and I didn't notice any coverings on them. They were just roughhewn, simple frames made out of stripped saplings, and seemed to be abandoned.

"Looks like whoever was here moved out," said Boo as we moved in closer.

"Yeah." I noticed that the former occupants hadn't been very tidy. There was assorted junk strewn about – plastic bottles, various food wrappers, a couple half-full garbage sacks, even a discarded, dirty sleeping bag laying by one of the old lean-tos.

I heard a grunt behind us, and whirled around, my hand on the butt of my pistol. It was just an old man, with a long, white goatee, climbing up from the riverbank.

"Who are you?" he asked us, a little breathless, his dirty Levi jacket hanging loose on his skinny frame. "I don't want no trouble."

"Don't worry," I told him. "We're just looking for a guy."

"You ain't cops, are you?" he asked, keeping his distance.

"No."

"Well good luck," he said. "Everybody's cleared out of here except me."

"Do you know a guy named Mike Maloney?" Boo asked him.

"Aww, shit, him," he said. "Cops ran him off a while back. What do you want with that shitbird?"

"This guy?" I walked over and showed him the photo, pointing out the Corporal, wanting to be sure we were talking about the same man.

"Guess so," he said, squinting at it. "Yeah," he added after a second. "Got the same scar across his chin. That's him."

"Know where he went?"

"Up by Index is what I heard. Who cares?"

"We care," I told him. "Up by Index, where?"

The old man narrowed his rheumy eyes. "Important to you, huh?"

"What do think?" Boo told him, not happy.

"Well, you know," the guy said. "I got to move, too. Mayor himself told me to get lost. I could use some help with moving expenses."

"Fuck that!" Boo took a step toward him.

"No," I told Boo. "Sure," I said to the man, then pulled a twenty out of my wallet, and showed it to him. "How's this for your move? Trade you for a better description of where Maloney went."

He grabbed it out of my hand. "Sure, bud," he said with a smile that was lacking a couple front teeth. "Up by Index. That's the north fork of the river. You pass the bridge into town and keep going. Maybe a mile, mile and a half or so. You'll see an old iron gate at this dirt turn-off on the riverside. Trail leads in from there. I've been up there myself before, long time back. 'Course nobody'll go up there when that fuck head's around. He's somewhere in that forest. Good luck. He's dangerous."

I knew we wouldn't get any more out of the man. Said thanks and left him to pack up whatever little he possessed.

"I wouldn't have given him shit," Boo told me as we retraced our steps back up the rocky, overgrown trail toward the car. We'd only gotten part way, when my cellphone rang. I pulled it out, and lost my balance a bit, recovering just as I answered it. It was Rachel.

"What's up?" I asked, getting my feet planted firmly again.

"I'm sorry about Smitty, Matt. Where are you? Where's Boo?"

"Up near Sultan, looking for Maloney."

"Oh, that's right. Did you find him?"

"Not yet. We've got a lead. About to track him down as we speak. So, what's up, anyway?"

"I want a gun and I want to learn how to shoot it," she told me.

"What happened? Something happen?"

"Someone I know got killed, maybe because of me. And I've been threatened. Comes with the job, I know, but I want to be able to defend myself."

"Thought I'd never hear you say those words," I said. "When should we do this?"

"How about tomorrow morning?"

"Sounds good." I gave her the address of the motel and told her to meet me and Boo there first thing in the morning.

"Take care, Matt. Don't do anything foolish or dangerous."

"Same-same," I said, clicking the phone shut, as I looked up, trying to place the sound I heard.

The sound became a loud *ker-whumping* that filled the air above us. Then its source suddenly appeared over the trees. Startled, I jerked my head around following it– saw a helicopter flying over us pretty low – its rotor blades making their distinctive *ker-whump, ker-whump* sound as they chopped the air – knew it was a Huey, like we used in Nam. As it passed, I twisted around, then stumbled, and the ground rushed up to meet me…

…I was on point again. My third time in three days. Alone in front of the platoon – only forty feet ahead of them, but it felt like a mile. All my senses were ramped up to the max. I moved quiet as I could through the jungle, step after careful step, attuned to the slightest noise or any trace of movement around me.

Then, ker-whump! I didn't really hear the explosion, just felt it; the shock wave making me feel like Jello that had been dropped on the floor.

Then, silence. Blissful calm.

Above me, a cascade of pinkish-red petals fluttered through the emerald green foliage. A lime-green snake slowly intertwined with a rust-red vine high above. White clouds in the deep blue sky played peek-a-boo above the jungle canopy. Canary-yellow birds flitted toward the tree tops. It was beautiful, so lovely I wondered why I hadn't noticed it before.

"Rossiter!" came a voice that sounded far away. "Rossiter," the voice repeated. I struggled to my feet. "You OK?"

"I was," I said, my legs all rubbery.

"He's fine." It was Sgt. Rivers walking up to me. He said it without even checking me out first.

"What happened?" I asked.

"Land mine," said Rivers. "Took out the new replacement, just knocked you down." Then he made a sour face and stepped back from me. "Christ almighty!" he told the other guys who'd gathered around. "This fucking cherry crapped his pants!"

"No shit," said Baker, also backpedaling.

"What a stink," said Coleman, putting a hand over his face.

Laughter when I realized that Rivers was right.

"Lose that load and clean yourself up," ordered Rivers. "We're moving out."

"I don't want to move out," I said.

"It was just a helicopter, Matt."

"What?"

"You fell and hit your head, dude." It was Boo – he was trying to get me to my feet.

"What?" I asked, my head hurting and spinning while he got his arms under my shoulders, trying to boost me up. I could still see the pinkish-red petals and the pretty yellow birds.

"Try to stand up, man. Help me out here," Boo told me.

I looked up – slowly realized that the pinkish-red petals were salmon berries – I must have tripped and fallen into them. The canary yellow birds were actually Boo's bright yellow Hawaiian shirt…

"That's it. You can do it," said Boo as I struggled to get up.

…and the lime-green snake was really a lime-green caterpillar hanging down off one of the salmon berry tendrils…

"Smells like shit," I said.

"Yeah," Boo told me, getting me upright and bracing me, my knees weak and wobbly "It's shit all right!" He pointed down at a big pile of crap next to the salmon berry bush. "Some asshole took a dump right next to the trail. You believe it? You almost fell right into it."

At least it wasn't my shit, I thought, really glad I hadn't crapped my pants.

"Can you walk?" Boo asked me. When I nodded my head, he said, "Good. Let's get you back to the car. You'll be fine."

"We've gotta get after Maloney."

"Not in your condition, dude," Boo said. "You've got a concussion. It'll just have to wait until tomorrow."

"What a bunch of shit!" I said, and then said it again as Boo helped me up the trail and my head all foggy and swirly. "Bunch of shit…"

Chapter Twenty-two

Rachel was pretty shook up when she showed up at the motel the next morning. Someone else had died the night before, the lawyer she was working for, and she was scared. We decided that Boo would teach her how to shoot and I would go and do some recon on the guy she thought was behind it all, a guy who used to be a King County Sheriff.

I was still feeling pretty spacey from the concussion. Or maybe it was from the four aspirin and the bottle of Wild Turkey I downed the night before.

The address Rachel gave me was in Shoreline, a suburb north of Seattle. The house was a split-level on a wide cul-de-sac. All the homes were perfectly kept except his, which had a front yard that looked like it hadn't been mowed for months, dandelions and weeds everywhere.

I was just figuring out how I was going to contact him, when he strolled out of the house, and walked up to his car, which was parked almost to his garage at the back of the driveway.

I piled out of the Firebird and stalked after him. He didn't hear me coming, was fiddling with the garage door handle when I blindsided him with the butt of my .45. Down he went. Didn't make a sound. Not until I rolled him over, sat on his chest, and stuck the barrel of my Colt all the way back to his tonsils.

He made a gurgling sound. If his wide eyes could talk, they'd have made a gurgling sound, too. As it was, I told him something that made his eyes get even wider, and his gurgle even louder.

"Fuck with my friend, Rachel Stern, again, I'll pull this trigger next time. You won't know where – you won't know when – but it *will* happen, asshole. Got it?"

He nodded meekly and weakly. I cocked the .45 just to add extra emphasis to what I'd said. He let out a little squealing noise, quivering when the hammer loudly clicked back. When I got up, I noticed he'd peed his pants.

Back inside my car, I thought it a lesson well taught. This chicken-shit bastard would never fuck with Rachel again.

I was pleased. So pleased that I drove over to the small Roanoke park, overlooking that area's McMansion houseboats, and treated myself to a drink. Had my windows rolled down against the heat, my Wild Turkey, and Smitty's memoir on the seat beside me, still unread. It was quiet; peaceful. I had something else to look forward to hooking up with Boo, and getting to Index to find the corporal. Maloney had to be our man. He was the only one left from the squad who was unaccounted for. But why would he have done all the killing?

Truth be told, I was long past 'why?' Corporal Maloney was an asshole, like Rivers, like Benny Luc. Some people were just born assholes, and 'why' didn't amount to shit. It was like asking why over fifty-thousand soldiers had to die in Nam. No use. We'd just hunt the bastard down. If we found out why, fine. If we didn't, tough shit.

Since I was on a roll, I picked up Smitty's memoir. Took another pull on the Wild Turkey, placed the memoir against the steering wheel for easier reading, and opened it up somewhere around the middle.

'It wasn't all bad over there, once we even had a BBQ, the memoir started. 'I remember we were somewhere between An Loc and Phuc Vinh and we were coming back from a patrol and there was movement on our right flank, and we knew there weren't any friendly ARVN soldiers operating there and we all opened up thinking it was an ambush. We shot the shit out of that whole area, but there wasn't any return fire.

'When Rossiter and I were sent to scout it out we were so surprised I can't tell you. No Cong or NVA to be found, just this dead water buffalo that was shot full of holes like nobody's business. We laughed so hard and then we laughed even more because we'd been so pumped up and thought we were being attacked and it was just this stupid fucking water buffalo. Even Sergeant Rivers and the corporal laughed about it.

'Well I'd been a cook for a steakhouse in Santa Cruz and I knew about meat and I said why don't we have a BBQ, and everybody said that was a great idea, we'd only had C-rations for days. I butchered the buffalo right where it lay, well I only butchered part of it because there was so much of it and some of the guys built a big fire and I took only the most tender cuts of buffalo that I could get at and we put them on sticks and roasted them over the fire and even then the meat was tougher than hell, but it was so good that we wished we had some beer to go with it.

'A couple of the other platoons came over to where we were because they smelled that water buffalo cooking. They couldn't believe it and one of them said he wished he had some BBQ sauce for it. He was from South Carolina and they had the best BBQ sauce. I butchered some more for all of them and our Lieutenant was pissed, but he had some anyway. The other platoon's Lieutenants were pissed but they didn't complain that much. The Company Commander was pissed, but he ate more than anybody I'd say. The gooks who owned the water buffalo were going to be pissed for sure, but we were fighting for them and to hell with them if they couldn't spare one fucking water buffalo.'

That was pretty damned good, I thought. Smitty could actually write. If his entries were all like that one, I could even read another. I flipped ahead a few pages.

'There's one thing I'll never forget that happened outside Phuc Vinh. We were marching up the road, we hardly ever went up the main road because the VC would mine the roads to take out tanks and armored personnel carriers, but we were on the road for some reason and it was raining really hard and came around a bend and I couldn't believe what I saw. There was a troop of APC's and tanks ahead of us, they were angled off the road, one of them to the right, the next angled off to the left and so on, which is what they did if they came under attack so they could go after the enemy on either flank.

'They were actually on guard, one guy on their machine guns up top guarding all these naked soldiers on either side of the armor beside the road. I couldn't believe it, the men were all taking showers in that heavy rain, soaping themselves up just like they were in a shower back home What was so funny was you could tell who had been in Nam the longest, because most of them were tanned like Indians from the waist up, but their butts and legs were shark-belly white. It was quite a sight, all these soldiers naked as the day they were born being guarded while they showered by guys manning the machine guns on the big, hulking tanks and armored personnel carriers.

'Rivers said to take five and we fell out and smoked them if we had them and Rossiter, he'd only been with us for a week or so, he said fuck it, he stunk, and he tore off his clothes and joined the guys taking their showers and borrowed soap from one of them and got all lathered up. Just as he got all soaped up, the rain stopped. No rain at all anymore.

'So, there he was covered with soap and no way to rinse it off. He ran back to us, all of us laughing our asses off, and tried to rinse off with the water in his canteen. That didn't work too well, and he asked me and a couple other guys to use their canteens to rinse off and we said fuck that, we wouldn't have any water to drink.

'That's when Rivers said we had to move out. Rossiter complained, and Rivers said you dumb-ass cherry, you get your clothes back on ASAP and it serves you right. Poor Rossiter said it itched like a mother all the way back to base camp.'

Fuck me, I thought. I had to laugh. I'd forgotten about that. Don't know how I could have, but Smitty really nailed it. It had been a bitch at the time, but it was sure damned funny now! What a kick. I needed this. I should've read this stuff before now. I flipped some more pages ahead, actually looking forward to it.

'I've made peace with God about what we did over there. It ate at me for years. Sometimes I thought it was why I lost my legs. Payback for what we did.

'I drank and drugged for years. Felt sorry for myself. Then I started going to church. I confessed my sins. Repented. It was the first time I felt good for ages.

'I am forgiven.

'I send money to an orphanage in Hanoi every month. Not much. Don't have much. I send them twenty-five dollars on the first of each month when my disability check comes in. They even sent me a picture of one of the kids there. His name is Tran. He's now eight years old.

'Tran looks a lot like the kid we took into our hooch at base camp. He was an orphan, too. He could dance like crazy, that kid. He didn't dance too well to the Hendrix music Rossiter was always playing, but he really liked it and tried. Pretended to play an imaginary guitar, like they call air guitar today, and you'd think he was actually playing the Hendrix songs. They were his favorites. He also liked James Brown whenever Rossiter wasn't hogging the tape deck. 'Papa's Got a Brand-New Bag' was the one he did best. You'd think he was a little gook James Brown the way he got all sweaty and worked it and tried to sing along with the lyrics.

'I don't know whatever happened to that kid. This kid in Hanoi, him I can help. I still have nightmares about things, even though I know I'm forgiven.

'When I think about it, I… We did bad shit… Real bad shit…

'I just can't write about those things anymore… that's it… I'm just going to stick to the happy stuff. Yeah…'

Back to the real world… I tossed the memoir down, where it bounced off the seat and landed in a heap on the floorboard. At least it was good, while it lasted…

Chapter Twenty-three

Boo and I hooked up back at the motel. He told me that Rachel did real good. He'd given her a .38 Special; a revolver, so she would never have to worry about it jamming like semi-autos sometimes did.

She was a natural shooter. I should have seen her. Every bullet in the target right off the bat. He'd used the simple point and shoot method – don't take time to aim – don't jerk the trigger – just point and shoot. After a while, she was making tight patterns in bull's eye area at twenty-five yards. She wouldn't have to be any closer than that to defend herself most anytime.

Boo liked my story about the deputy. Said he'd be surprised if Rachel had to defend herself against him after what I'd done.

We had some lunch on the deck of a nice restaurant on the water. Took our time afterwards getting our gear together for hunting the corporal. Boo had everything we needed. Around mid-afternoon, we took off, both of us eager.

It was late in the afternoon by the time we found the iron gate up past Index. Thought it would be easier to find from the description the old man had given us. We must have driven by it three or four time before we finally spotted it. It was set back from the highway proper, deep in the forest in the middle of nowhere.

Only pushing 6:00 PM, it got dark early here in the mountains. The light was already starting to fade, and it seemed much later in the day when we headed into the woods in search of Corporal Maloney's campsite. We figured we had a couple hours before it got too dark, even though there were a lot of eerie shadows the further we advanced into the forest.

It was still hot out, somewhere in the high 80's. Everything combined to remind me of our Search & Destroy missions in Nam. The rifles we carried, the AR -15's that Boo had brought with him, civilian models, only semi-automatic, but looking just like the M-16's we once used. Our quiet and deliberate hunt for a dangerous enemy. The thick underbrush that could obscure a trip-wire or punji-pit; and the stress and sweat that ran down the back of your neck as you stayed hyper alert for any movement, especially in your peripheral vision.

A low mist draped the forest floor like it had many early evenings in Nam. Like those long-ago days, everything was still and quiet. Like the world had stopped, except for me on point, ahead of my platoon in the jungle. My body moving forward, but most of me caught in a slow-motion zone between life and death. My senses tuned to the max even though time stood still. Part of this zone was safe, nothing could hurt me because I wasn't there. The other part of me was caught between fight and flight. A never-ending limbo where I was all dressed up for battle with nowhere to go. My palms sweaty on my assault rifle, hearing sounds I'd never heard before, like the individual beat of a mosquito's wings. The fog on the ground might obscure everything from trip-wires, to other booby-traps like snares and punji-pits or land mines.

That's how it was hunting Charlie back then. And that's how it was again today hunting Corporal Maloney. Everything was so similar: the rifle in my hand; Boo right behind covering the flanks; slowly advancing into the fog-shrouded forest attuned to any movement and every sound. I had to keep reminding myself that it was 1999, not 1969. We were in the forest up past Index, not the jungle. This Charlie was one man, not a thousand faceless bastards out to kill us at every step. The mist swirling around our feet didn't hide punji-pits or other booby-traps, just pine needles and a few fallen branches.

Yeah, we could have been in Vietnam again, instead of the deep forest above Index. The only real difference was we weren't humping fifty pound packs, and wore camouflaged outfits rather than Army olive drab. I had to keep telling myself that. This this was different. *It is different, Matt, don't let it get away on you.*

For some damned reason, part of me liked it. God help me, I did, but didn't know why. Maybe it was familiar, something easy to relate to, 'been there, done that,' black and white. Not my life since the war, filled with memories I couldn't forget, fueled with drugs and booze that dulled them, but also magnified them.

Who knew? Maybe it was the adrenalin rush. I knew it worked for Boo. He was smiling as we worked deeper and deeper into the forest. Crazy-assed Boo, he couldn't have been happier to be back in the shit.

We'd gone about half a mile when Boo abruptly stopped and raised up his arm with a closed fist, meaning halt and stay quiet. He motioned me forward and pointed at the ground about three feet in front of him.

"Trip-wire," he whispered.

I slowly advanced; saw the wire stretched out dead ahead less than a foot above the ground.

Boo pointed up at the big Fir tree that towered over us. "Dead-fall trap," he whispered. Sure enough, there was wide log, maybe eight feet long, hanging from a rope attached to big limb directly above us. Trip over the wire and down the heavy log would fall, crushing anybody beneath it.

Damn. Booby-traps like this. Corporal Maloney was paranoid, like he was still in Nam. And he was making me paranoid, too… *I was not in Nam!* I was in the here and now.

But, I was right back in the shit, anyway – every step I took fraught with enough danger to set my heart racing even if I stood still. Boo told me once that he thought our infantry platoons were like bait – we were out in front, first to draw fire, then they'd call in artillery or air strikes to support us (if there was anything left of us, that is).

There was no artillery or air power to call on now. We were all there was. Just Boo and me – alone.

We carefully went around the wire. Stayed vigilant, though. Sometimes there'd be multiple wires: another one hidden close by, so if you spotted the first wire and avoided it and thought you were safe, the second wire would trip you up and bring death down on you anyway.

After a bit, we came to an area that was a complete tangle of underbrush. No use to try to go through it, so we went around. We trod as carefully as possible, but couldn't help making something crack or snap under our feet now and then, which set me on edge. Had we given away our position? Would somebody open up on us because of it?

We stopped and listened. Alert for anything. The forest, like Nam's jungles, was like a living being. When you really listened, you could hear it breathe. The river rushing in the distance was like blood flowing through its veins. It always made me feel that we were in the belly of beast, slowly being digested.

On the move again. Came to a path that had been tramped down through a wide growth of tall ferns which led up a slight rise. Probably an animal path, a trail that some type of animal always followed. We couldn't be certain. You found a path like this in the jungle, it was worth following – could be a Cong or NVA highway – and it could also be also be a set-up to draw you into an ambush.

We'd just started up the path, fern fronds on either side brushing against our legs, when we caught a terrible smell. It came from somewhere ahead of us: the all too familiar sickly-sweet smell of death and decay.

We followed the scent. We'd been all about death in Nam, so there was nothing else to do. Boo and I had lived death, breathed death, and brought death for so long that it was only natural to seek it out.

We were locked and loaded, ready for anything when we came upon the source of the smell. Boo stopped abruptly and motioned me forward, pointing out something just ahead of him.

I edged up and saw what it was: a punji-pit about two feet in diameter with a rotting porcupine impaled on the sharpened stakes at the bottom of it.

"Fucking porcupine," Boo whispered, then let out a small laugh and shook his head.

And there was that young soldier, no older than me, screaming bloody murder, fallen into a large punji-pit, wicked bamboo stakes driven through his right foot and straight into the calf of one leg, each stake a good foot and a half long.

We'd been on a sweep, other platoons operating about twenty-five meters on either side of us, when this poor bastard fell into the pit. I was closest to him and went over to see what was up. No sooner had I seen his condition and his buddies working to pull him out, than Sergeant Rivers rushed up to me and grabbed me by the shoulder.

"Get the fuck back in line, cherry," he yelled. "And learn a lesson. That troop will be dead in days. Gooks smear shit all over those stakes. Infection's going to take him no matter what they do."

"Trail's a trap. Corporal must have made it to draw people in," Boo quietly told me. "Let's get out of here."

Boo slowly backed up, protecting our rear, as I led the way out, the image of that young soldier still branded in my brain.

Finally back where we started, Boo said, "We must be getting close to his camp. He's probably put theses booby-traps all around its perimeter. That's what I'd do."

"Yeah," I said. "That's the case, we need to go this way." The two traps we'd come across were roughly parallel to each other. I pointed at the trail we'd just come from. "Bet his camp's somewhere over that rise."

"Yeah," Boo agreed. "Could be a bitch. Keep an eye out."

"I know."

I took the lead this time – Boo had been on point long enough – and led the way around the hillock where we'd found the dead porcupine. A couple hundred feet later we came to an area that had been logged off a great many years ago. It was full of huge, decaying stumps of first growth trees, many of them three and four feet across. Problem was that it was also thick with alders that had filled in after the big evergreens had been taken down. The alders were so dense in spots that you could hardly see what lay ahead. This was compounded by long strands of moss that hung down from a lot of the trees.

We halted and took our bearings.

Movement!

Our rifles came up at the same time. But it was only a squirrel taking a flying leap from one limb to another.

"Bullshit," said Boo, lowering his weapon. "This is like that damned rubber plantation we used to go through, dude. Whole lot thicker, though."

"Yeah." Boo was right – at least the rubber plantation had its trees planted in even rows, though slightly offset in a diamond pattern – you could see through them much better than these alders that had grown up willy-nilly everywhere. Still, though, Charlie or NVA could have popped out from behind those rubber trees any time at all, and they could do the same here, only easier. The thought was unsettling as the rubber trees were about the same diameter as many of these alders. An AK-47 round could go clear through a tree that size if you took cover behind one – something our smaller M-16 rounds couldn't duplicate.

"We should fan out," Boo told me. "Get a better look at all the angles if we get a little distance between us."

We went into the alders at the same time, but stayed about thirty feet apart, same as we'd done in the rubber plantation: I covered angles Boo couldn't see, and he did likewise for me.

That's when the birds stopped singing. Just like the war, they stopped and all was quiet – *and that was not good.*

I was tense. Even more tense than I'd been humping up that trail through the ferns. I knew we had to be close to his camp and that made it worse. Like Nam, nothing ever got easier – the damned alders harbored the thickest underbrush we'd come across, which made even better cover to hide more booby-traps. The way everything was mostly in shadow from the dense trees, made it that much tougher.

It stayed that way until we got completely around the rise and the land became fairly flat again. Still couldn't see much through the alders, and had to zig-zag some to avoid much of the taller underbrush and foliage, but at least we'd hadn't run into anymore traps.

Boo stepped on a dry branch that made a loud crack as it snapped. I froze, then saw him hit the dirt. I instinctively followed suit, wondering what he might have seen. Boo raised up slightly and pointed dead ahead. "There he is!" he said in a loud whisper. "See him? About forty meters out; up against that tree!"

Took me a second, then I saw it – a human figure standing right next to a tree; looked almost like he was leaning back against its trunk. There was just enough light piercing the shadows, or I might have missed him.

Boo assumed a semi-kneeling position and raised his rifle. "I'm going to take him out," he told me, clicking off his safety.

"Hold it," I said. "He's too far away – I can't tell if that's Maloney or not."

"Shoot first; ask questions later," said Boo like he was in the Wild West.

"We'd need scopes to tell at this distance," I told him.

"Gotta be him, man. Who else would it be?"

"We want him alive, anyway. Find out why he—"

"I don't give a shit 'why,'" said Boo, grudgingly lowering his rifle. "Fine. OK. Let's move up, get a better look. But he's dead the second he points a weapon our way."

We crawled forward, quiet as possible, taking advantage of all the cover we could. I lost sight of the Corporal a few times as we slowly moved forward, the forest floor sometimes smooth, but often rough and prickly against our bellies. Each time I paused, and the Corporal came back into view, he didn't seem to have moved. I wanted him as bad as Boo, but I had to know why he did what he did.

At roughly twenty meters to our quarry, we hunkered down behind a large stump with suckers growing out its top. I glanced around its base and saw his figure more clearly, though it was still partially obscured by the alders and hanging moss. He hadn't moved a bit, seemed to be holding a wide log to his chest that was about as long as his torso.

"That's Maloney all right," said Boo, from the other side of the big stump. "What the fuck's he holding?"

"I can't tell."

"Let's get a little closer," Boo told me, smiling wickedly like he always did when he was having fun. "He moves, we rush him."

We worked our way forward another five meters. The Corporal remained stationary, now appeared to be sandwiched between the tree at his back and the log he held. But the closer view point also showed that he wasn't actually holding onto the log – his arms were hanging loosely down at his sides.

"Fuck it!" yelled Boo. He jumped to his feet and charged. "Remember me, asshole!"

"Don't shoot him!" I followed Boo quickly as I could, but he had a good twenty-foot lead on me. By the time I caught up to him, he was standing in front of the Corporal, but had his AR-15 harmlessly pointed at the ground.

"Doesn't need to be shot," Boo told me. "Look at this shit. He's already toast, dude."

"Damn," I said, looking at the Corporal in disbelief. The log he 'held' was actually another type of deadfall trap, only this log was covered with sharp, foot-long wooden spikes that now dripped with the man's blood. It had swung down from a limb above the Corporal and pinned him against the alder as surely as butterfly collectors pinned their specimens to their collecting boards. The wooden spikes had penetrated deeply into his chest and abdomen, and held him tightly upright.

"Haven't seen one like this since that time outside Phuc Vinh," said Boo. "Remember?"

I didn't want to remember.

"Caught in his own trap," Boo added. "Very cool."

I studied the man's face. Contorted in death as his pallid, almost gray features were, he was Rivers' hatchet man, no question. Gained some weight over the years, sure, but still had his wild shock of wavy blonde hair and the scar that went through his deep dimple as it crossed his chin. His ice-blue eyes had the same unfeeling, cold stare that they had when he was alive. Looking into them again for the first time in so many years made me shudder and want to turn away. I forced myself to touch the skin of his face and neck. He was still fairly warm. This hadn't happened that long ago.

"I don't get it," I told Boo. "He must have known where he placed all his traps. How the hell could he have walked into this one?"

"Might be an answer here, Matt." Boo had gone to the far side of the body and picked something up. "Look at this." He held out a pistol for me to see. It was an Army model Colt 1911 .45 caliber semi-auto, same type that I always carried.

"Check it," Boo continued, pulling the magazine out of the gun. "Empty. Nothing in the chamber, either."

"Give it here." I knew Boo was right, but I checked it anyway. Then I smelled the barrel – it had been fired recently.

Boo slowly walked away in the direction that the body was facing. Then he bent down and picked up a shell casing. "See this?" he asked me, then went a couple paces forward. "And this?" he asked again, picking up another shell casing. "Look," he pointed at the ground ahead of him. "There's a trail of brass leading up to his body. I'd say he was chased into his own trap – emptied his clip at whoever was after him, and backed right into it."

"But who—"I started to say.

The air filled with loud music, blaring almost to the point of distortion.

It was 'All Along the Watchtower,' by Jimi Hendrix.

Chapter Twenty-four

The trail of shell casings pointed in the direction that the music was coming from. Boo and I stood stock-still, listening and looking for any new danger. All we could see in that direction were more densely packed alders – these grown so close together that the upper foliage of each tree touched its neighbor's spread of leaves, making a thick canopy like we so often encountered in Nam. In short, there wasn't much light. It was just twilight and dark shadows ahead.

"Somebody knows we're here," said Boo. "That music didn't start by itself."

"Yeah," I said, listening to my all-time favorite Hendrix tune and wishing I'd never heard it.

"It's just like you said, dude: this joker leaves a Hendrix calling card with every one of his kills."

I didn't respond, kept glancing right and left, then behind us in case the music was a ruse designed to focus our attention in the wrong direction. Saw nothing, though; was only aware of the song calling for me to follow it.

"Saddle up, Matt," said Boo. He slapped the bottom of his ammo clip, making sure it was fully seated in his rifle. With a nasty smile, his eyes fairly glowing, he started forward. "Search and destroy, man," he told me. "Search and destroy."

We went in side by side, the music growing louder with every step, the hair on the back of my neck standing up, my palms moistening with sweat.

Everything about it said ambush! I'm on point again. Sweat dripping down my neck – my hands so sweaty it's hard to hold onto my M-16. Only my third patrol – my third patrol in as many days. I can't get Ashcroft's severed head still in his helmet out of my head. That's how it is – any minute blown away – face frozen with its the last expression. I'm a cherry – a green cherry – "you'll ripen, cherry," says Sergeant Rivers – yeah, I'll ripen, maybe even burst open with my guts hanging out like the soldier I saw on my first patrol…and I never even knew his name…

Then it happens! One minute, just starting to get more comfortable – the next, utter fucking chaos! I'm eating dirt, face down – bullets whizzing so close I can feel their 'zip and whoosh' cutting the air – how they miss me, I don't know – our M-60 machine gun chatters and buzzes through the jungle ahead of me like a hedge-trimmer – and this VC comes at me out of nowhere!

…he's on top of me – trying to choke me – and it's all going dark – I get the bayonet off my belt and sink it into his stomach and slash it down toward his groin with both hands…

…his guts spill out onto me – he groans and collapses on me – I push him off – the air fills with the stink of shit – his shit – out of his intestines – on me! – good God Almighty, on me!

…then it's quiet – no more shooting – no nothing – the VC had hit and run --and Boo Riley pulls me up and says, "good for you, cherry, we're going to get those gooks" – and I'm on my feet and we all charge after them…

…I'm running, but I'm not here – I'm floating like a ghost – I'm so high – better than being stoned – I'm alive! – so alive – never felt better – I'm fucking Superman!

…and we come to that village…

…we know the Cong went into that village...

…and we go into that village…

"Matt." It's Boo, he's tapping me on the shoulder. "You with me, dude?"

"Yeah," I tell him. For a minute, I'm not – and then, I am. "Yeah, I'm with you."

"Good. I think we're close."

We're deeper into the darkest part of the woods. The music was now so loud it almost hurt my ears. The song ended, then began again like it was on some sort of endless loop.

"Look up ahead. See that light?"

I focused and saw the light he was talking about. It was visible through all the tree trunks maybe twenty meters or so in front of us.

"Looks like a clearing up there," Boo told me.

"You're right."

"Hey, check it," said Boo. He pointed at an alder, slightly off to our left, about fifteen feet from where we stood. "There's big speaker mounted there."

"Sure enough," I said, as we walked up closer. Partially obscured by some leaves, it was fixed to the tree, a couple feet higher than our heads, where a big limb branched off from the trunk. A long brown extension cord led down to the ground and snaked off toward the clearing.

"Who the fuck's doing this?" Boo asked me.

"Wouldn't be here if I knew," I told him. I thought of Benny Luc for a second, but that was crazy, he'd been in jail when all this began. It was obvious that it wasn't Corporal Maloney, so I still didn't have a clue. "Whoever it is," I said, "good bet this cord will lead us to him."

"Maybe straight into an ambush," said Boo. "We're the ones who need to do the ambush. Let's split up and turn the tables." He gestured to the left. "I'm going to work my way up there and try to flank the bastard. You keep going on ahead. Either of us makes contact, we should have him between our guns. Sound right?"

"Good as it gets."

"OK. Give me a little lead-time, though. A few minutes. I'll go out thirty, forty meters, then turn toward the clearing. Nothing's hit the fan by then, you go for the clearing, too."

"Got it."

Boo nodded the affirmative, then flashed me the biggest grin I'd ever seen. He turned and started away from me, saying, "What a blast!"

I checked my watch, marking the time. As I waited, I wasn't exactly feeling Boo's joy. I felt more like a watch that had been seriously overwound. There'd be time enough for happiness, if and when we got this guy. In the meantime, the Hendrix song booming in my ears, all I knew for certain was that we had left the watchtower and gone to meet the enemy.

After the minutes ticked off, I started forward, Nam's jungles and this forest all threatening to merge into one. The heat, the traps, the bloody dead Corporal – it was same-same, but it wasn't. *I knew where I was*. If you needed to depend another soldier, it was Boo Riley: fucking madman killing-machine who laughed while he worked and always had the best dope.

Still, though, I couldn't help but hear LBJ's oft repeated words as I approached the clearing: "My fellow Americans, there is light at the end of the tunnel." I hoped he was right this time, because he sure as fuck wasn't right last time. I can still hear him on Armed Forces Radio: "My fellow Americans, I will not seek, nor will I accept the nomination for President."

Hippies and flower-power and free love ruled while we died.

Twenty meters doesn't seem that far – a little over sixty feet – but it was a lifetime following the extension cord that I thought would go on forever.

What's to worry, though? Can't see him, but Boo's a hundred, hundred-and-twenty feet off to my left – I've got fire support. I moved up and stopped, still in cover, just a few feet from the clearing.

It was green and lovely. A long, rectangular swath cut out of the forest. Dappled by sun and a few puffy white clouds. It was tall, wild grass, polka dotted with red, white, and blue wildflowers – the kind of place that deer loved to graze. Just like the clearing that Amazing Grace and I had made the most magical mescaline-fueled love in once upon a time. I was her, and she was me, and we were so together. It was as far away from Nam as you could get.

Today, Nam was waiting for me in the clearing. The extension cord led to large speaker and tape-deck sitting on a stump no more than thirty feet from the edge of the woods. Jimi kept playing as I scanned the area. As far as I could tell, the clearing was empty, not a soul in sight. Just Hendrix singing over the pastoral scene that was dotted here and there with big old growth stumps and many smaller stumps, probably alders harvested for their hardwood.

I couldn't stand there forever. I wasn't going to step into the clearing and expose myself to fire, either. This was where it would end. That damned speaker sat on the stump like some kind of bait. I wasn't going to take the bait. Since our platoons were like bait, then the point-man was *really* the bait – expendable, a human trip-wire, worthless until he got experienced – that's why Rivers put me on point so much. I'd learned. Boo had helped me learn. I had full faith that Boo was covering my ass right now, but I still moved with extra caution.

I stepped sideways to get a better view, still keeping some cover. Normally I'd be listening for the slightest sound, but Hendrix's song drowned out every sound but his own.

I scanned right and left, saw no movement, nothing, fully aware that somebody could be crouched behind one of the big stumps – even the one with the speaker on it.

I moved sideways again. he ground gave away beneath my feet!

My rifle went flying as I fell!

Next thing I knew, I was three feet deep in a big punji-pit!

The worst pain I'd ever felt shot through my left foot and up my calf…

…I looked down…

…saw a narrow wooden stake driven completely through the arch of my foot...

…saw another stake that had missed my right foot by less than an inch…

…twisted and groaned as I tried to pull my foot of the stake…

…blood spurting everywhere…

…couldn't do it…

…searing, electric, hot pain…

…stuck half in and half out of the ground…

Movement to my right!

I drew my pistol, but somebody's foot kicked it out of my hand just as I brought it up.

An Asian man stood over me. Vietnamese. He had an AK-47 aimed at my chest. He wore jeans and a plaid shirt. Biting down against the pain so hard I thought my teeth would break, I realized that he looked very familiar.

"Remember me?" he asked.

"Yeah," I said at length. "You're Mr. Nguyen. I met you at Benny Luc's trial."

"No," he told me. "I'm Charlie."

My head was spinning. I felt like I'd pass out.

"I'm *Charlie,*" he repeated.

He was confusing me. "You're no Charlie," I said. "We called the Viet Cong Charlie. You're a businessman."

He took a step back and frowned, looked sad for a moment. "I *was* Charlie," he told me.

"What the fuck are you talking about?" I felt like I was going to throw up.

He squatted, kept the rifle aimed at me. "Little Charlie. Don't you remember?" he asked. "You liked to watch me dance. You would put on a tape and I would dance."

It slowly dawned on me. I remembered him dancing like he didn't have a care in the world. "My God…" I said.

"There is no God," he told me. "There is only justice."

"You're the little boy we took in."

"Yes. That Charlie."

"But how—"

"I was sad, and you made me feel better," he continued. "You and the other soldiers called me Charlie. I learned later it was insulting. But you were the only soldier who was really nice to me, Matt Rossiter. When you went back to America, you gave me your tape-deck and your Jimi Hendrix tapes. Do you remember?"

"I do," I said, still hardly believing that this was Charlie after all these years.

"When the Americans left, and the Communists took over, I found my way to a refugee camp in Thailand. As the years went by, I mostly forgot about you, thought only of reaching America. When I did, I became fluent in English, went to U.C. Berkley and earned an M.B.A. I came to Seattle and started my business. Then you came into my life once again. Last year, remember? When our Vietnamese community honored you for taking down Benny Luc and his gang. I could not get you out of my mind after that. It took time, but I managed to secure a copy of your old platoon list."

"You wanted revenge."

"Justice," he said, standing again.

"I'm sorry," was all I could manage. Very woozy, I began to feel extremely chilled, even though it was still hot outside.

"Yes, justice," he told me. "I survived, but my mother did not," Charlie went on, his cadence measured. "Neither did my sisters. Nor my grandmother. Nor my cousins. Nor my aunt and uncle. Nor my father – you see, he had been murdered by the Viet Cong two weeks before you came because he refused to cooperate with them."

The last part of what he said tore into me as bad as the pain in my foot – *the VC had executed his father…*

The irony of it just shook me to the core: his father wouldn't help them and they had executed him *weeks before* we had gone into that village…

There was nothing to do but surrender to my fate. It had been a long time coming. My eyes were full of tears, and my heart was filled with more pain than it could hold. The way I felt, and had felt since Nam, I knew I'd be better off dead.

"There's been too much killing," I said.

"Yes."

I raised my hands and stretched out my arms. "Shoot me," I said. "I deserve it."

Boo popped out of the woods, bringing his rifle to bear, about fifty feet away from Charlie.

"No!" I shouted.

"Boo!" he yelled, firing at the same time.

The bullet caught Charlie in the side. He spun halfway around, lost his grip on the AK, and fell to the ground face-first, just inches from me. I didn't have the strength to keep standing, and started to sink further into the pit, every inch causing new waves of agony through my skewered foot. I managed to stop my descent by placing my arms across the lip of the pit for support. This put me face-to-face with Charlie.

I thought he was dead, but his eyes slowly opened, staring directly into mine. Like me, he must have been in terrible pain, but he didn't make a sound. Then he surprised me by reaching out and taking my hand in his own. He squeezed it tight. When I squeezed his in return, he smiled. For a second, his warm brown eyes were those of the sweet little seven-year old who craved attention and danced up a storm to James Brown and Jimi Hendrix.

Then he was gone.

"What the fuck?" It was Boo. He stood over Charlie's lifeless form. "What the hell did you mean yelling 'no' at me? This gook was going to kill you!"

"He's Charlie," I said.

"Charlie?" said Boo. "He's no Charlie."

"No," I said, the world starting to spin and go black. "Don't you get it? He was Charlie."

"Dude," Boo told me. "He's no VC. This isn't Nam. You're delirious." He looked down into the pit at my foot. "Fuck," he said. "Hold on. I'll get you out of there."

Epilogue

Three weeks later, I couldn't get Charlie out of my head. Or his village either. Benny Luc was still out and about, gunning for me, I was sure. The prosecutor was threating to charge me with perjury, and I told him, "Prove it." There was talk about trying to revoke my PI license. Life was great.

Tanaka was pissed. The head found in Rivers' locker was never fully explained. Turned out it belonged to some biker from Vancouver, B.C. Sometimes you don't always figure everything out – Rivers kept ears from Nam, so why not heads?

Jessica Ito came to see me. She hadn't spoken to me since I left her in the lurch. She knocked on the door to my motel room and I said I was glad to see her, but was occupied. She pushed the door open a little further just in time to see Amazing Grace come out of the bathroom toweling her hair dry, but not wearing a stitch. So that went well.

Anyway, I'd rented a room at the same motel on Eastlake that Boo and I had stayed in. A few people had offered to let me stay with them, but I wanted to be alone. I liked the Eastlake location because it was just a few blocks away from where my houseboat had been. There was a little pocket-park by the water where I'd sit and watch the contractors rebuilding the floats for my new houseboat. I had full replacement coverage through insurance, and my rep said the houseboat itself should be rebuilt before the end of October.

I also found a new duck family while I watched them work on my houseboat. The ducklings were a lot bigger than the ones I'd lost, but they also had bigger quacks as they went after the bread I fed them. I was sure they'd still be around when my houseboat was finished.

So, all in all, I was in fine shape, except for the nightmares I'd had for years. It's funny – Rivers used to occupy them a lot, and even though he was dead, he was still the same bad actor who came on stage with great regularity. I had plenty of Wild Turkey to counter him. It didn't work as well for Charlie, though. Same-same for his damned village, but that had always been the case.

What wasn't good, however, was coming back to my room and finding an unexpected crowd inside it. Tanaka, Boo, Rachel, Amazing Grace, and even Jessica Ito were there (although Jessica and Amazing Grace sat as far apart from each other as they could in my small room). Oh, yeah, and there was some guy in his early-40's – receding hairline, stocky, with a ruddy complexion – who introduced himself as Mike Baldwin. He gave me a small smile when he shook my hand, but seemed very serious, like a man on a mission.

In fact, they all seemed like people on a mission. After a few pleasantries, they got right down to it.

"Your friends are here today," Mike told me, "because they all care deeply about you."

"Fine," I said. "What's up?"

"In fact, they are very concerned for you," Mike continued.

"Who wants a drink?" I asked, my radar starting to track where this shit was going.

While I grabbed the Wild Turkey from the T.V. stand, Boo said, "It's true, dude."

Tanaka, who had been fiddling with his tie, which he often did when nervous, said, "I've known you for a long time, Matt, and you know I do really care about what happens to you."

"You rehearse that line, Dale, or what?" I asked him, taking a slug right out of the bottle since nobody else seemed to want a drink.

"He does care about you, Matt," said Jessica. "We all do."

"Hey, buddy," said Tanaka. "You know me. I don't say anything I don't mean."

"Babe," said Amazing Grace, coming over and putting an arm around me. "People love you. Take the love."

Jessica quickly followed suit; sat next to me on the edge of the bed, and put a hand on the top of my thigh. "She's right," she told me. "You need help, Matt."

I stood up. "Thanks, but I don't need any help. I've still got money in the bank, my foot's healing up fine, and I've got a place to stay while they rebuild my houseboat."

"You know what we're talking about," said Tanaka.

"Yeah, you're trying to pull some damned intervention on me."

"Matt," said Mike. "Your friends—"

"You don't know me," I told him. "And I don't know you, so—"

"I've known Mike for a long time," said Tanaka. "He's helped a lot of vets."

"Great," I said.

"Dude," said Boo, coming up to me. "Just listen to what he has to say."

"Sure: I drink too much and I've got P.T.S.D. I've heard it all before."

"Admitting it is the first step," Mike told me. "You're right – I don't know you. But I've known hundreds like you."

"Mike's a P.T.S.D. counselor at the V.A.," said Tanaka. "He's pulled some strings and gotten bed-space for you in their in-patient program."

"I've already got a bed," I said.

"We have both group counseling and individual counseling in the program," said Mike. He handed me a glossy brochure with the V.A. logo on it. "I won't bullshit you, though. It's tough – things will get worse before they get better – but they *will* get better."

"I *am* better," I told him. "So I see no reason to get worse."

"Matt," said Tanaka. "Be honest. You *have* gotten worse. Especially after the shoot-out with Benny Luc's gang last year. You've been zoning in and out ever since then."

"I don't know about that particular firefight," said Boo. "It's true, dude. When we were out in that forest together, me, I was just having fun, but you were in-country again. You were a living flashback. You really thought you were in Nam half the time."

That much was true, but I didn't say so. Instead I said, "Well, I suppose this is when you all start telling me how much you love me again and try to break me down so you can haul me off to the VA, right?"

They did just that.

Have to admit, I got a little misty-eyed, especially when Grace said she always knew I was full of some secret sorrow, and had an empty space inside me that sex and drugs couldn't fill.

Then Boo started in about our history together. How he met me in Nam; how, just out of high school at only eighteen, I was the youngest in our platoon, and how he felt like throwing my Hendrix tapes out because I played them too much; talked about our various patrols and firefights…

…and I started zoning out as he kept going on and on about our time together during the war…

…and by the end, all I could see was that village burning behind us as we left, could still see all the bodies piled up in its small courtyard, and couldn't shake little Charlie's face, happy to have a place to stay, happy to clean all of our jungle boots for one crappy pack of Juicy Fruit, happy to police the hooch for us, happy to have plenty of C-rations to eat, happy to dance, and us never knowing that he was from the village we'd annihilated…

…but worst of all, I kept seeing Charlie's eyes while Boo continued to talk; eyes that were warm and bright, but changed when woken from his frequent nightmares to ones haunted with awe and wonderment at his world gone mad, a world without reason, one of sudden death and loss, terror and carnage that he could not understand.

I broke down and started crying – blubbering like a baby, actually. Boo and the others held me and hugged me and tried to comfort me like I often did with little Charlie.

"I'll give you a ride to the VA now," said Mike, putting a gentle hand on my arm.

I managed to salvage some dignity. "No," I told him. "I'll take myself there tomorrow."

"Matt…" said Jessica.

"Matt…" echoed Tanaka.

"You really should go now," Mike told me.

"Not happening," I said.

"Half the people who say they'll go on their own never go," said Mike, not just talking to me, but addressing everyone.

"No worries," I said, using a tissue that Amazing Grace had pulled out of her purse. "I'm a big boy; I'll get there in the morning."

"You sure?" asked Tanaka.

"Hey," I told him, still wiping my eyes and nose. "I didn't go through all this drama just to cop out."

Everybody let out small laugh at that – all except Mike, that was.

Rachel, who had been very quiet, said, "If that's what Matt wants."

"Good enough for me, dude." Boo gave me more of a hand slap than a handshake, then added, "Be there or be square, huh?"

"Right," I said.

There was a pregnant pause, all of them wondering if it was over or what. Normally I would've asked either Jessica or Amazing Grace to stay, but I didn't want any company. Instead I said, "Well thanks, everybody. It means a lot that you did this for me."

Taking the cue to leave, each of them gave me a hug or a kiss or a handshake, then went out. Mike, the last to leave, turned at the door and said, "Remember, Matt; if you don't show up, it's a bed-space that could have gone to another vet."

"Got it."

He nodded, then left.

Finally, alone again, I communed with my Wild Turkey for a long while, thought about my friends and lovers, then went down to the lake to see if my new duck family wanted an evening snack – told them I'd be gone for a time, but to stick around, I'd have plenty of bread for them when I returned.

The next morning, I told the manager I was checking out, then went outside and revved up the Firebird.

The sun was shining brightly as I hit the entrance to the freeway, the Space Needle and downtown Seattle just glimmering as I headed south toward the VA hospital on Beacon Hill.

The Firebird's 500-plus horses purred smoothly while my head swam with the events of last night, and everything that came before – Rivers, my squad, that damned village, Charlie – everything that always caused me to wake up drenched in sweat, the bed sheets kicked all over hell and back, whether it was summer or winter, spring or fall.

I didn't feel like listening to Hendrix anymore. Nearing the exit to the VA, I put a new tape into the deck, then fast-forwarded to the Beatle's song that had always played in my head when things got too rough: *Strawberry Fields Forever*.

My cellphone rang. I tossed it out the window, uncapped my bottle of Wild Turkey and began to sing along. The familiar lyrics comforted me. I floored it, punched the Firebird to over 100 mph and left the VA far behind.

END

About the Author

Curt Colbert is a Vietnam vet, who is also a poet, an avid student of history, and a boxing fan. He has written three hardboiled, historical PI novels set in Seattle in the 1940's, the first of which, Rat City, was nominated for a Shamus Award. He was the editor of Seattle Noir, an anthology of noir short stories set in Seattle. In addition, under the penname, Waverly Curtis, Curt co-authored five humorous mysteries in the Barking Detective series with his writing partner, Waverly Fitzgerald. Curt lives in the Seattle suburb of Mountlake Terrace with his understanding wife, Stephanie, and under the thrall of their somewhat demanding cat, Miss Kitty. Curt is presently working on the next book in the Matt Rossiter series, *Strawberry Fields Forever*.

CPSIA information can be obtained
at www.ICGtesting.com
Printed in the USA
LVHW091817281119
638726LV00014B/2323/P

9 781941 890684